Th

A novelization by Leonore Fleischer
Based on the screenplay written by
John Brancato & Michael Ferris

First published in Great Britain by
Boxtree Limited
Broadwall House, 21 Broadwall, London SE1 9PL

10 9 8 7 6 5 4 3 2 1

ISBN 0 7522 0138 7

A CIP catalogue record for this book is available
from the British Library

Cover design by Shoot That Tiger!

Phototypeset in Sabon by
SX Composing Ltd, Rayleigh, Essex
Printed and bound in Great Britain by
Cox and Wyman Ltd, Reading, Berkshire

1

The sudden rattle of gunfire from an oversize assault weapon was followed less than a second later by unearthly screams. Blood and brains spattered everywhere, dark scarlet mingling with grisly grey. More shots, more shrieking, even louder this time; the exploding gore more vivid and even . . . wetter.

Angela Bennett leaned closer to get a better look. The expression on her face was absorbed, even fascinated. Bodies were falling right and left, but that didn't break her concentration. All her attention remained focused on the screen of her computer. Above the non-stop action of the sadistic and violent CD-ROM game its name flashed over and over: Wolfenstein XII. The graphics were excellent, Day-glo good guys and baddies virtually leapt off the screen; the colours were strong and the sound effects convincingly scary. Wolfenstein XII was going to make a bundle at the cash registers, if this puppy could ever get out of the techno-trouble swamping it.

Angela's computer, a high-speed state of the art setup sweetened by every major add-on the industry afforded, was her bread and butter, her main squeeze, the love of her life, her number one reason for living.

She had three of them, three beautiful babies linked together electronically, but each terminal could operate independently of the others. She worked at home, right in the living room of her own small house, as a sort of super-analyst trouble-shooting consultant for Cathedral Software, which was what she was doing right now. Fingers on her keyboard, Angela leaned closer to the pulsating screen. Three more good guys exploded, their digital heads blown to smithereens by the bad guys' superior killing power.

'This is a very ... dynamic ... game, Mr Depina,' Angela said into the air.

The voice of Hubert Depina, manufacturer of Wolfenstein XII, was taut with anxiety as it rasped out of the speakerphone on the desk next to the computer. 'Be honest. It's violent smut. Its only purpose is to make a buck. The kids will eat this up, but only if you can find out what's crashing the damn thing.'

Angela nodded, staring intently at the screen, and her fingers hit three more keys, one at a time. She waited a few seconds, a small furrow appearing between her eyebrows as her large dark eyes narrowed in concentration. 'Diplomacy's for free. My advice is what you pay for.'

'And your advice?' squawked the speaker fearfully.

Biting her lip, Angela touched the Escape key gingerly. The instantaneous result was catastrophic. The screen seemed to erupt in a blaze of light, and the characters — humans and aliens alike — began to crumble away, pixel by pixel, and disappear in a scene of mass destruction until the screen was almost blank. It was a massacre, exactly what she expected, but being right in this case didn't make Angela Bennett happy. She scowled at the dissolving screen.

'Don't even think of hitting the Escape key on *any* of your systems for a while,' she said in the direction of the phone. 'One keystroke will wipe out your whole system.'

'Oh, God,' moaned the manufacturer, and the young woman could hear the genuine wretchedness in Depina's voice even through the distortion of the speakerphone.

Now Angela, not daring to breathe, went to work in earnest. Her dark red hair, long and loose, swung around her face as her eyes darted back and forth, intent on the computer monitor. As she scanned the changing screen, her face glowed. Her slender fingers began to fly across the keyboard until they were a blur. Having diagnosed the virus, she had to move really fast to find a cure for it before it became fatal, a 'terminal illness', she thought to herself with a wry grin at the lameness of the joke. One after another, her keystrokes yanked down diagnostic windows, which she eyeballed at lightning speed, the clicking keys making instant choices. Inspecting, testing, Angela Bennett chased the destructive virus across cyberspace until she cornered it like a cat corners a mouse. Mouse, right. Double-clicking her mouse, she froze the screen. At once the images stopped disintegrating; the pixels still on the computer screen remained there. Gotcha. Like a hunting cat, Angela Bennett really enjoyed the chase, the exhilarating sense of power when she brought down her kill. And, like a hunting cat, Angela was very efficient at catching her prey.

Angela Bennett let her breath out in a whoosh. 'Well, you've been virused, Mr Depina, and not such a nice one. It could've knocked out everything in its path, and it was activated by just hitting the Escape key. But it's all under control now; it's going to be okay.' She took a bright red blank diskette from a box of them, and slipped it into the 'A' drive, hit the Copy key and began downloading the insidious virus on to the backup disk, as though injecting a biological virus into a test tube.

'Oh, God, oh, God,' moaned the speakerphone, and Angela Bennett could picture the client wringing his hands. 'How could this happen? I took precautions. I even ordered a security program last week, what do they call it, Gatekeeper?'

Angela grinned, revealing strong white teeth framed by full shapely lips. 'Did you get around to installing it?'

Silence – a meaningful silence – from the speakerphone. Then Depina admitted, 'I don't think we received it yet.' Angela's grin widened.

'Is it remotely possible that we'll have everything back to market by week's end?' begged Depina.

'Everything but the virus,' she reassured him, and pulled the red backup disk out of the drive. She wrote out a label for it: 'Depina Delete Virus,' and drew a little skull and crossbones to drive the warning home. The computer virus which had attacked and nearly destroyed Wolfenstein XII was now safely captured on the diskette, an evil genie shoved back into its bottle prison. 'The guy I work for collects them,' she said, sticking the label on the disk. 'I dunno, some people save string . . .'

'You are a goddess, a merciful angel from above,' crooned the grateful Mr Depina.

'You may feel different when you get the bill from Cathedral Software,' chuckled Angela, her swivel chair turning to one of her other computers, whose screen was lit and prompting colourfully. She began typing briskly.

'Whatever you want! Take! But you must grant me the honour of painting the town red this evening – '

'Mr Depina, I'm flattered and appreciative,' she interrupted.

' – Oysters, champagne?' persisted the grateful dis-embodied voice.

'But unfortunately I already have dinner plans,' said Angela, hitting a few more keys.

'Then tomorrow! The next day!'

'I appreciate it. I wish I could, truly,' Angela lied. 'But these plans, they're kind of a . . . a standing arrangement.' She made her final choice from the menu of options, clicking her mouse. Anchovy double-cheese, ordered from Pizza.net, her credit card information already punched in. Her standing arrangement, large regular crust pizza to go, would be here in forty-five minutes. The screen said, 'Thank you, Angela Bennett. Gratuity not included.'

Only hours before Angela clicked her pizza choice

into the Net, three thousand miles away in the nation's capital clear across the country from Angela Bennett's little house in Venice, California, an important man was making an important telephone call on his cellular phone. He had never heard of Angela Bennett, and as things would work out he never would, yet this single telephone call and its consequences would be instrumental in changing the course of Angela's life forever.

The man on the phone was Undersecretary of Defense T. Michael Bergstrom, and his rugged features were crumpled in anguish as he pressed the instrument even closer to his ear.

'There's no chance a mistake could have been made, a mis-reading?' he pleaded, his deep voice breaking. 'Human error? It happens – ' He listened for a heartbeat, while his face fell further. Whatever the news he was receiving from the other end of the line, it was really bad news. 'Oh,' he said finally, dully. 'Well, that sort of rules that out, then, doesn't it?' Bergstrom's voice dropped to a near-whisper.

'Mr Secretary, you car,' said a voice close by. Bergstrom looked up, distracted.

'Excuse me?' He blinked, almost surprised to see his driver Eddie waiting deferentially near the late-model black Lincoln town car. The undersecretary nodded absently, acknowledging the car. 'Ah, yes, thank you.' Walking slowly down the steps of the Federal office building, Bergstrom snapped the cellphone shut and stowed it away in his jacket pocket.

Eddie said nothing more, but the look on his

employer's face puzzled him. Michael Bergstrom was a man of great vigour and physical stamina who always walked swiftly and surely, but now he was moving like an eighty-year-old, and his face looked grey, his eyes shadowed with something very like fear. The driver opened the back seat door, and Bergstrom slipped inside. Eddie closed the door with a sharp click and climbed behind the wheel. The powerful Lincoln purred away from the curb. As it stopped for a light on Pennsylvania, Mike Bergstrom said quietly from the back seat, 'Let's take the parkway, Eddie.'

The parkway? Another surprise. The boss was usually in too much of a hurry to bother with the longer, more scenic route. But he *was* the boss, so if he wanted the parkway, the parkway was what he'd get. Eddie shrugged and made a left turn.

It was a lovely, tree-lined drive along the Potomac. At this time of day, just before evening drifted in, Washington appeared at its most enchanting. The white marble of the magnificent presidential monuments and memorials, the Capitol Dome, the awe-inspiring public buildings – all glistened in the late afternoon sunlight and cast long shadows; the tall obelisk of Washington's Monument looked down on its exact duplicate in its reflecting pool. For the next ten minutes the Lincoln moved along quietly at fifty-five. Mike Bergstrom rolled the tinted windows down so he could look out at the view, and smell the sweet-sour riparine smell of the Potomac. Up ahead was a roadside fruit stand.

'Eddie,' Bergstrom called suddenly. 'You know what I'd like? Stop the car.'

A minute later the car started up again, and Bergstrom was now holding a perfect ripe pear in his hand, his senses engaged in enjoying its shape and colour, its fruity perfume.

The fruit-stand owner watched dumbfounded as the Lincoln disappeared. He looked from the car to the greenback in his hand, and back again. 'You see that?' he demanded of his brother-in-law, who helped him out at the stand. 'Goddamned guy just gave me a hundred bucks for a lousy pear!'

'Republican,' snorted the other man in disdain.

At Bergstrom's instruction. Eddie turned off the parkway toward the river and stopped the car. Warming the pear between the palms of his hands, the undersecretary got out and strolled to the water's edge. Sighing, Eddie settled down to wait for his suddenly unpredictable boss. He took a folded newspaper out of his jacket pocket and turned to the sports section.

Dusk was falling, that sad sweet time of the evening between daylight and dark, and the lights of Washington were coming on, shimmering in the river like nearby stars. Taking a bite of the pear, Bergstrom pulled out his cellphone again, and dialled his home, talking to his wife for a few moments and then getting twelve-year-old Mike Junior on the line. They talked for a minute or two, the older man savouring the sound of his son's eager voice.

' – okay, buddy, final offer. Non-negotiable. For every buckle-down hour you give Algebra II, you get two hours of quality time with Nintendo and Sega.

10

Deal? Just whatever you do, don't tell your mother. Good. Now, put her back on.'

While he waited for his wife Elizabeth to come back to the phone, Bergstrom took another big bite out of the pear and chewed it. It was juicy and flavourful, and it filled his entire mouth with its sweetness. He shut his eyes, totally savouring the taste of the fruit. Then he heard his wife's voice, and he swallowed hastily. 'Okay, hon, number one son back on the strait and narrow. Me? Fine. Just needed a little field trip to clear the head. Bit of a nightmare day. I'll see you in a bit. You bet. . . . I love you, Liz.'

Slowly, Undersecretary of Defense T. Michael Bergstrom shut his cellphone, and put it down on one of the picnic tables that dotted the riverside park. He reached into his pocket and pulled out something . . . something about the same size as a phone, as hard, as shiny, but infinitely more deadly.

There was only one bite of the pear left, and Mike Bergstrom chewed and swallowed it. Then he raised the .38 revolver to his head and placed the barrel into his empty mouth. In the gathering darkness Eddie's eyes strained to see the baseball scores in his tabloid newspaper. He almost didn't hear the shot.

Back in Venice, Angela Bennett's standing-arrangement pizza had come and was now gone, little more than a crumpled box stained with tomato sauce and holding only a few leftover slices and the dry crusts. Time for dessert. Angela peered into her refrigerator, which yawned back emptily. A pint of milk, almost on the turn, a piece of fruit, half a head of lettuce, a nearly empty jar of cocktail onions, a stemmed glass getting cold, and a small aluminium can. She grabbed up the can. It was a pre-mixed Martini cocktail. Dessert, her one and only drink of the day. More than one made her tipsy and less inhibited; Angela cherished her inhibitions and preserved them with care. Popping the tab on the drink, she poured it into the chilled glass, pried a little onion from the bottom of the jar and chucked it in. Now the Martini was a Gibson. Pawing through her extensive CD collection until she found her favourites, Angela put a handful of them on the record changer.

With Annie Lennox purring 'A Whiter Shade of Pale' softly out of the speakers, Angela settled down at her computer with her drink, enjoying the first cooling sip. With her right hand she held the glass, with her left she logged on. A few keystrokes and she was on the Net, mouse-clicking toward her bulletin board. The Internet was Angela Bennett's drug of choice, her relaxation, recreation, the focus of her free hours. As Cyber Chat, her bulletin board, came up on the Net screen, she smiled broadly. Angela's teeth were healthy and white and even, thanks to good genetics, a diet rich in calcium – double cheese on her pizzas – and a little judicious orthodontistry when she was in grade school. When she smiled, those teeth dazzled, and it seemed as though this strong, vigorous young woman was going to take huge bites out of life.

But Angela Bennett didn't take bites out of life, she

barely nibbled life at its edges. Whatever fears dogged her and prevented her from intermingling with her fellow humans, she had never really defined them. But they were there. As a computer systems analyst and expert in software trouble-shooting Angela had found a comfortable reclusive niche, and stayed in it happily, like a snail too vulnerable to come out of its shell. She worked alone, which she preferred. She worked at home, the only place she felt really protected. She had no hassles of office politics to contend with, no sexual harassment in the workplace. As a freelance systems analyst, she didn't have to go out into crowds, into the shoving, noisy, smelly company of others, into that vortex of their overwhelming pushy self-confidence that sucked the marrow from her bones. Angela Bennett had turned telecommuting into a fine art, reaching out only by speakerphone, modem and the FedEx courier who brought her deliveries and took away her pickups. Otherwise she stayed pretty much holed up in her little vintage bungalow near the Grand Canal, behind a high wooden fence that kept the rest of the world out.

So she had withdrawn from life as most everybody lived it, leaving the human community, creating instead an environment in which she felt safe, a comfort zone bounded by terminals, screens, diskette, modem, mouse, software she could hide behind and preserve her anonymity. Anonymity gave her a sense of freedom. She spent hours every day at her keyboard, on the Internet. Angela Bennett was turning into a computer geek, a cyberhead, whose only friends were hackers, nerds and geeks like herself, the faceless population of the Net, men and women she hadn't ever met and no doubt would never meet. Just pixels on a screen, with nutty identifying icons and call-name pseudonyms, like truck drivers on CB radio. These were the cyberpeople she held conversations with, exchanged opinions with, made jokes with. These were her chosen relationships.

Which was a shame, because she was such a pretty girl. If she'd only fix her hair, which flopped into her eyes, and wear better clothes than those flannel shirts and jeans she was addicted to, she'd be a *very* pretty girl. Why not? Only in her middle twenties, Angela was blessed with a lean, supple figure and a beautiful complexion, and a cleft in the point of her chin that gave her face an arresting quality. She had thick, abundant auburn hair that waved naturally and eyes large enough to star in a velvet painting. Angela had every raw ingredient for real beauty . . . except one – confidence.

But Angela Bennett didn't get her hair done because she couldn't stand the idea of a stranger touching her, a pair of strange hands shampooing her head, another pair of strange hands cutting the hair and shaping it, a stranger making trivial, gossipy conversation with her while all this was going on. For the same reason she never got a manicure or a massage or a facial. She couldn't bear the idea of a shopping mall, so Angela kept clothing shopping to a minimum, and wore her old clothes until they went into holes. Hey, they kept her warm in the winter, cool in the summer, and

14

covered her nudity. What more could you ask from clothes?

Besides, of what use was a perfect figure to a young woman who walked around tentatively, as if her sneakers were crushing eggshells, hunched over a little as if to hide her shapely breasts and rounded hips from prying eyes? Who would ever see that thick hair and those huge eyes or experience that lovely smile? Angela Bennett was not unlike Wordsworth's poetical heroine Lucy, about whom he wrote, 'A Maid whom there were none to praise and very few to love,' or perhaps Angela was closer to the lines from Thomas Gray: 'Full many a flower is born to blush unseen and waste its sweetness on the desert air.' The desert air on which Angela Bennett's sweetness was wasted was the Internet.

The Internet. Nobody owned it, everybody used it, and all you needed was a computer with a modem and time on your hands. The Net had started out more than twenty-five years ago, as Arpanet, a network of computer systems set up in 1969 by the Advanced Research Projects Agency, 'Arpa' of the US Department of Defense. The idea behind Arpanet was to keep the lines of communication open in case the Cold War turned into a hot one and there was a nuclear attack on America. If part of the system was damaged in the attack, the rest of the system would continue to function. During the next decade, the network had grown slowly but steadily as other computer networks joined up with it. In the Eighties, universities began to link up their research departments with the expanding Net, making scholarly data

15

accessible to students and teachers hundreds – even thousands – of miles away. Eventually, the Cold War over, Arpa dropped out of the Net, which is now maintained by The National Science Foundation and other organizations, and commercial users began to link up and log on. Today, more than two million computers are on the Net and probably more than fifty million users, and it's growing faster every day. It's estimated that the monetary value of the Net is now more than three billion dollars, and that's just for starters. There's no telling how valuable it could become in the future.

Point and click. Now Angela was in, right on her chat line, reading the messages left on the Net by the online buddies with whom she was used to chatting nightly. Iceman had written: 'No one leaves the house anymore. No one has sex. The Net is the ultimate condom.'

Angela grinned; not too shabby, worth a reply. She quickly typed in her own Net call name, 'Angel', and followed it with, 'That talk Iceman could lead to eventual extinction of R species.' Her own voice came out of her computer speakers, digitalized and disembodied. One of the stranger qualities of the Internet chat lines and bulletin boards was the weird sound effects.

Someone else chimed in on their conversation, Cyberbob. 'My sympathies exactly Angel – let's have a date and procreate,' he offered.

The competition pissed Iceman off. 'C-Bob,' growled the computer screen, 'you wouldn't know a sympathy from a symphony or your ass from a *Whole Earth Catalog.*'

Gandalf 361, self-named for the wizard in the J.R.R. Tolkien novels, identified him/herself: '86 the language, Ice – cybercops are listening. You'll get us all tossed from the Net.'

Cyberbob was back. 'Cybercops, techno weenies, hackers, crackers, thought police, Big Bad Wolf – what large ears they have, Grandma.'

'Paranoia overload,' typed Iceman. 'Got to sign off, mother's calling. Talk to U all in a few days.'

'Not me, Ice,' typed Angela, taking another sip of her canned cocktail. 'In two days I'm off on vacation. Just me, a beach and a book.'

'I'm there, babe,' drooled Cyberbob. 'Look no further.' His message was followed by :-), geekspeak for a Smiley Face, which became obvious if you gave your computer (or your head) a turn to the right.

Angela laughed out loud. 'Sorry, you're the best, Bob, but not my type.'

'I'm crushed,' came the typed reply. 'So what do U want in a man?'

Everything, thought Angela. As long as I'm dreaming, make it a good dream; nothing less than everything. She typed, 'Butch, beautiful, brilliant; Captain America meets Albert Schweitzer. Spends all day dashing into the fray, fists flying, making the world safe for democracy; at night playing Bach cantatas while curing cancer.'

The cursor on her screen blinked while Cyberbob thought about his answer. Finally, these words appeared: 'Settle for a guy who puts the seat down?'

'Face it Angel,' put in Iceman, 'yer dreamin. Yer one of us.' He typed her a little computer Frownie Face, :-(, a symbol of his sympathy for her situation.

'We accept U,' agreed Cyberbob. 'We accept U one of us one of us.'

Angela folded her hands in her lap. Suddenly her face lost its glow and her eyes darkened with loneliness. 'Yeah, I know,' she whispered.

With only two days left before she would take off for the Yucatan, Angela found she had things to do. Not a lot of shopping for clothes; she already had a perfectly usable two-piece swimsuit not much more than three or four years old, and it would never occur to her to buy a new one. When she'd told the other cyberheads on her chat line that it would be a book, a beach, and herself, she wasn't exaggerating. All Angela wanted was to get away on her own to a non-crowded resort in the off season, where she could sop up the sun, and sit quietly and read undisturbed.

Still, even Angela, who wasn't bothering to bring along her camera on vacation, or buy film, had shopping to do. She took herself to the supermarket, where she moved through the aisles swiftly and uncomfortably, avoiding eye contact with other shoppers and making no impulse buys, just sticking to her list. She stocked up on a fat-free frozen lasagne dinner, another can of pre-mixed Martini, plus its accompaniment – a new jar of cocktail onions, a large can of Almond Roca, and a bottle of p15 sunblock.

When she got to the front of the 'Ten Items or Less'

line, Angela put her few purchases on the belt and stood quietly as they were rung up. Everything passed the computerized bar code scanner except the sunblock; the plastic bottle didn't light up the light-emitting diode screen above the register.

'Price check on two!' the cashier bawled; he was a sullen, pimpled, shaven-headed youth with six earrings in his right ear.

Nobody came for the price check. The store managers were all busy somewhere else. Angela glanced behind her nervously. The line for the register was growing longer, and the people on it didn't look happy at the holdup.

'I'm still waitin' on a price here,' the cashier growled at the line.

'Oh, for Chrissake!' exploded the man next in line, his limited patience already wearing thin.

Angela couldn't handle this. This was exactly the kind of irritated human confrontation she always tried to avoid. Her cheeks began to redden with embarrassment. 'Forget it, forget it,' she told the youth. 'I'll risk the burn. Just total the rest, please.'

'$19.55.'

Taking out her ATM card, Angela swiped it through the debit-pay machine. A second or two later, the terminal chirped and 'Hello, Angela Bennett,' read out on the LED.

She grabbed up her small package and ran to her car. Once behind the wheel, she drew in a deep breath and let it out slowly. No question about it. Even the smallest daily public transactions were getting harder and harder for her. She was really ready for this vacation.

But one important duty remained before she was free to go. She had to see her mother in the nursing home.

Although she was only sixty years old, Mrs Bennett suffered from Alzheimer's Disease. Angela had cared for her at home as long as possible, but the bitter day eventually arrived when it would no longer be possible, when her mother's condition had worsened to the point that she needed around-the-clock professional care. The decision to put her mother into a nursing home was the hardest decision of Angela's life, even though she knew that it was the best thing for both of them. Once her mother had been moved, Angela's last daily contact with loving human interaction had been severed. Angela's own life shrivelled up a bit more, and she closed her petals around herself even more tightly, like a flower shrinking from the too-hot sun.

As nursing homes go, Oaktree Manor wasn't a bad one, it was even rather pleasant, but realistically no nursing home is the Ritz Hotel. They are filled with the elderly, the old, the infirm, the delusional, the abandoned, and they are the last stop before the final destination. The only way out is a hospital bed or a pine box. Seeing her mother there always tore Angela to pieces. She wanted to snatch her up, run with her to her car, and drive her away from there at sixty miles an hour.

Her mother didn't seem to mind Oaktree Manor.

Her memory had deteriorated to the point where her surroundings almost didn't matter. She was lucid enough, but had no complete memories of other times, other places. Little wisps of the past blew across her atrophying brain like swift-moving summer clouds, but they formed no complete picture of a life.

Angela made her way into the home's small lounge, which was filled with the elderly at their quiet pursuits, some playing cards, others bingo, a group of white-haired women in wheelchairs watching a home shopping show on the lounge TV. She found her mother at the piano, where she spent much of her time. In her former life, she'd been a piano teacher.

The illness that had robbed Mrs Bennett of the memory of her music had left her the use of her fingers. As she sat at the keys, although she believed she was playing as well as ever technically, she was actually only banging out one or two discordant notes. Today she thought she was playing a nocturne. One key hit, again and again.

Angela sat down next to her mother on the piano bench. She looked at the sheet music. 'It's beautiful,' she smiled. 'I love Chopin.'

Mrs Bennett paused and looked vaguely at Angela. 'You know this piece?'

'Of course. You taught it to me.' Reaching into her bag, she took out the large can of Almond Roca. 'I brought you something. Here – and this time, don't let the nurses eat them all.'

Her mother's hand reached out eagerly, grabbing the candy. She leaned over and whispered to Angela,

'My favourites, dear. How did you know?' She took out a piece and began to nibble it, looking curiously at Angela, whom she didn't recognize.

How did I know? Oh, mom! No matter how long her mother lived, Angela would never get used to the fact that she didn't recognize her own daughter any more. She knew it was a common symptom of Alzheimer's and that she mustn't take it personally, but Angela couldn't help the feeling of rejection that went through her like a knife every time her mother looked at her with a blank stare of non-recognition.

'Let's try this piece together,' she said quietly. 'The next part goes like this.' Angela picked up the nocturne from the sheet music and began to play the Chopin. After a few bars, Mrs Bennett put her hands on the keyboard and tried to play along. Her face wore a look of intense concentration as she tried to recall this music which sounded so familiar and yet unfamiliar to her.

Later, the two of them walked hand in hand in Oaktree's garden. The garden was not an elaborate one, but it had palm trees with broad leaves, bright yellow marigolds which will grow in any climate, red and pink geraniums, colourful ice plant spreading across a larger bed. The sun was shining, and quite a few residents were out enjoying the warmth, a number of them on walkers. A large tiled fountain was splashing water.

'I'm going on vacation for a while, a trip to the Yucatan,' said Angela patiently. 'Now, Mom, please listen. I don't know if there will be telephones where I am, but I'll talk to the nurses. If you need to get hold of me for any reason – '

'You . . . you must be one of my students?' faltered Mrs Bennett, peering at Angela.

Angela couldn't help flinching, and a look of pain came into her eyes. It had been many weeks since her mother had stopped knowing who she was, but it still hurt terribly. 'No, Mom, I'm Angela,' she said quietly. 'Your daughter.'

Was there a glimmer of momentary recognition? If so, it passed as quickly as it came, leaving Mrs Bennett's face with its usual expression of confusion.

'Oh . . . could you . . . bring me candy next time? My favourites are – '

'Yes, Mom, I know.' *I know.*

With less than twenty-four hours before her flight, Angela sat down at her terminals to tie up a few loose ends. She was online with an airline service on the World Wide Web, confirming her reservation and requesting a bulkhead seat when she heard her name being called at the screen door.

'Angela Bennett?'

She turned, tried to make out the figure standing there.

'FedEx!' he identified himself.

Meeting him at the door, she signed for the express envelope. 'Thanks. And here's another one going back.' She picked up the red Depina virus disk with its label decorated with the skull and crossbones and got out an envelope pre-addressed to Dale Hessman at Cathedral Software. Dale was really going to enjoy adding this one to his collection. The FedEx man watched her as she put the disk into the mailer and handed it over.

'Nice place,' he remarked pleasantly as she sealed the envelope. He looked around the small neat yard.

'Hmmm?' Angela responded automatically, only half listening. 'Oh, yeah. Thanks.' She held her hand out; he let the receipt go and grinned at her. 'Have a nice day.'

As the FedEx man went through the open gate, Angela spotted her neighbour Mrs Raines peeping at her curiously while she stowed her kitchen garbage into a large can by the kerb. Angela didn't socialize with any of her neighbours, keeping her privacy behind her high fence, so they were all nosey about her, especially the Raines woman. Catching Angela looking back, she scurried into her house.

Angela grinned and shook her head, prying open the Cathedral Software envelope as she went to her terminal. She pulled out a single mini disk labelled 'Mozart's Ghost Net: by Dale Hessman, property Cathedral Software, Beta Version: For Testing Purposes Only!!!' Stuck to the disk was a yellow Post-It, and on it, in Dale's handwriting, 'Weirdness here!! Call ASAP. Dale.'

Weirdness? A grin spread across Angela's face, lighting it up. She loved a challenge. She slipped the disk into the A drive and sat down at the keyboard. The program began to load, and a classic painting of Wolfgang Amadeus Mozart's face appeared on the screen, while the opening bars of *Eine Kleine Nacht-musik* came from the computer speakers, played on the harpsichord. Suddenly, the music changed into a heavy metal riff, a bolt of lightning on the monitor and the image of a guitar-playing skeleton appeared, and with it the words 'Mozart's Ghost'.

'You've just hit the Mozart's Ghost Net,' said the skeleton, 'the ultra-mega-major web server that'll access your head to *everything* about the hottest band on the Internet – '

'Nice to meet you fellas,' smiled Angela. 'Now, give me your best weird . . .'

She began typing with one hand, moving the mouse with the other, pulling down Ghost menus one after the other. Graphics scrolled across the screen; icons for photos of the band members; concert information; a fan chat line; a download for a selection of their music; an interactive sales line for ordering CDs and cassettes, posters, tee shirts, logo baseball caps and concert tour jackets. Angela pulled down more windows. So far, only normal merchandising, no weird.

'What's up with this? Gotta call Dale. Without taking her eyes off the monitor, Angela hit the speakerphone and jabbed the speed dial button for Cathedral in San Francisco.

'Cathedral Software,' announced an operator's voice.

'Dale Hessman, please. Angela Bennett calling.'

'One moment, please.'

As Angela waited to be connected, the open phone

line played a commercial for Cathedral over and over. A voice, friendly but canned, told her that Cathedral was 'a company that provides personal software for the World Wide Web. Fitness, Finance, and Fun . . .' Angela had heard this perhaps a thousand times, and paid no attention to it now, waiting for Dale.

Then, Dale Hessman's deep voice came over the phone, chuckling. 'Hey Angela! FedEx ship software had you signing for that disk three minutes ago. What took you so long?'

'I was fooling with this disk,' grinned Angela. 'I've also sent you a whopper of a virus for your hall of fame. Careful with the Escape key. So tell me, who or what is Mozart's Ghost?'

'Angela!' Dale's tone was a mix of amusement and exasperation. 'They're only the biggest thing since the headbanger craze!' He waited for some response, and got none. 'Don't tell me you don't know about head-bangers. You really need to get out more.'

'I have to get out to get headbanged? I'll stay at home, thanks.'

'All right. Different strokes. Look, here's the problem. Pop yourself into "Concert Information".'

Angela found the correct icon and clicked her mouse. For an instant her monitor screen seemed to shimmer, then it flashed to something entirely foreign – the main menu of Houston Utilities. She blinked in surprise.

'Houston Utilities – boy, did *you* make a wrong turn.'

'Not quite Ticketmaster, is it?' laughed Dale. 'Now, see anything unusual?'

Angela's eyes narrowed as she peered at the screen. 'Seems like a normal Web page . . .' She spotted something. 'Except for some icon at the bottom of the screen.' It was tiny, a little Greek letter, pi, π.

'Click on it,' Dale said.

She tried it. No change. 'Big nothing – ' she began, and then, in one sudden burst and with a strange popping noise, the screen came alive. Images crowded one another so quickly that their visual assault almost blinded Angela. One after the other came a series of schematics, wiring diagrams, account numbers, grid patterns – what the hell was going on here?

Suddenly, a shrill electronic beep sounded an alarm and the screen erupted again, returning to the Mozart's Ghost main menu. Angela blinked, and sat back in her chair. She drew in a deep breath. On first thought it seemed to her that this must be the most thorough example of cracking of a protected computer system she'd encountered since Kevin M., the notorious hacker, had been arrested and sent to jail for breaking into and raiding a number of corporate networks, pilfering telephone numbers to gain access to computer systems, stealing credit card numbers, and breaching the electronic guard of a topflight Japanese computer security specialist company based in San Francisco. Who could have achieved this? A cracking job like this one would take real techno-smarts. The work of a pro, or at least a semi-pro.

'Dale, I thought your cracking days were over,' she accused him playfully.

'I'm good, but not that good,' came crackling out of the speakerphone. 'So, whaddya make of all this?'

Not a cracking job? Angela thought a moment. 'Simple,' she said at last. 'You got a programming glitch, a futzed keystroke somewhere that sent you to the wrong Internet address. That's all.'

But Dale had more to tell. 'It sent me yesterday to Amtrak's central mainframe, and then the Mayo Clinic – neither of them in Houson, by the way – and last night it brought up an AT&T switching station in Omaha!'

Whoa, this was something else! Angela had never encountered a breach like this one before. 'Okay, you win,' she conceded. 'It's weird. Why don't you just climb in there, find the program error and delete?'

'I'm not quite ready to do that yet. Tell me what your day's like tomorrow.'

Tomorrow? No way!! 'Oh, no, Dale, no no, noooonnnnoooo,' she begged with panic rising in her voice. 'Don't do this to me. I'm going on my first vacation in six years. I just confirmed it, no refunds allowed.'

'What time's your flight?' he persisted.

'Noon on the dot. But I've got to pack, I'm going to be a madwoman . . . can't it keep till I get back?'

There followed a long pause, and Dale said finally, 'Don't think so.' There was a heaviness in his voice that surprised Angela.

'What? Russ on to you about the convention coming up?'

'Constantly . . . but that's not it.' Dale sounded really bummed.

'You want to tell me what this is all about?'

'I'd rather not on the phone,' he answered. 'Look, I can fly down tonight, be there by breakfast. We'd have five hours. Angela, you know this shit better than anyone – ' Dale Hessman pleaded.

Angela could not remember ever hearing him plead before. Dale was always so cool and laid-back. And what was the vital importance of a virus in Mozart's Ghost? This was only a rock and roll band, not a missile silo. But she was torn between her wish to help him out, and her need to be on that plane to Yucatan at noon tomorrow. Also, she found it hard to say no. Then, too, her professional curiosity, the weight of a new challenge, tipped the balance in Dale Hessman's favour.

'All right,' she gave up with a sigh. 'I'll see you at seven.'

'Great, great!' Dale sounded very relieved. 'So, we finally get to meet. I'll be the tall guy.'

Tall. That's exactly how Angela had always pictured Dale. Tall and thin, dressed in jeans and a flannel shirt, sitting in a cubicle in a crowded high-tech office with old Fillmore posters on the wall – The Airplane, Big Brother and Janis, Jimi, the Dead – and surrounded by the latest hardware and software. It was a dead-on mental image. Cathedral Software was cutting edge, a large corporation, but it was largely staffed by tekkie refugees from the Sixties, with massive and convoluted cyberbrains.

'Fine,' she said to the speakerphone. 'I'll be the one with Spineless Simp tattooed on her forehead.'

Dale Hessman filed his flight plan from San Francisco

to Burbank, where small planes were allowed to land. He allowed for an hour's drive in a rental car from the San Fernando Valley to Angela's house in Venice, so his estimated arrival time at the Burbank airport was just before five in the morning. An experienced pilot with more than a thousand flying hours on his log, Dale was at the controls of one of Cathedral Software's private aircraft, a sleek new four-seater Beechcraft Bonanza prop plane.

It was still at least thirty minutes before daylight when the banks of Avionic Read-Outs on Dale's computerized instrument panel told him he was well into his landing approach.

'Burbank Tower, this is Bonanza Two-Niner-Yankee commencing final ILS approach on runway eight,' he said into his headset radio.

'Roger, two-niner, runway clear,' the tower radioed back. Dale began to lower his landing gear.

'Ah, two-niner?' The flight controller's voice crackled through the radio. 'We should have you on radar by now; what is your position and altitude?'

Not on Burbank's radar? Puzzled, Dale checked his control panel. The Glide Slope Indicator was working normally, the middle light was blinking red and beeping reassuringly. 'Just passing the Middle Mark towards runway eight at 600 feet – '

'That's a negative, two-niner,' the tower interrupted. 'You're just not there. I'd check your instruments – '

What the hell did he mean, 'not there'? The Bonanza was at five hundred feet now, and giving up altitude with every second. The gear was down, he didn't have time to retract it now. Dale fought back a rising fear. 'All normal! For cryin' out loud, you must be able to see my lights – '

'That's a negative, too. Why don't you pull up and try again?'

Probably the best idea, thought Dale. Better safe than sorry. 'Everything looks okay, Burbank, but – '

'Ohmigod! Shit! Shit!!'

Dale Hessman broke off in horror as he looked through the windscreen and saw, dead ahead of him, four 1,000-foot smokestacks that were not supposed to be there. Nothing like it in his flight path. But there they were, looming, deadly. Desperately, he tried to pull up the plane's nose, but it was too late. He barely even had time to scream as the small plane ploughed into the first two stacks, shearing off its wings.

A moment later, at the second set of stacks the Beechcraft Bonanza turned into a fireball and the wreckage blew out of the sky.

In the split instant before he, too, exploded into smithereens, Dale Hessman suddenly understood exactly who had done this to him and why and how it had happened.

2

It was now fifteen minutes to eleven. Angela's plane to the Yucatan was scheduled to take off at noon, but all passengers were asked to arrive at the airport at least half an hour in advance of their flight-times. It was totally unlike Dale Hessman, she thought, to stand her up like this, without so much as a phone call. Dale was usually so reliable; she always thought of him as calm, mellow, rock-solid. Stowing her luggage in the trunk of her car, she kept glancing anxiously at her wristwatch. Angela had been consulting her watch every minute and a half for the last quarter of an hour. She couldn't delay much longer; Yucatan and the beach were waiting for her. She'd give him another few minutes. Besides, she really wanted to take one more look at Dale's disk, at that puzzling virus in Mozart's Ghost. Shutting the trunk, she went back into the house.

Aware of every minute passing, knowing that she was taking a chance on losing her flight and the vacation she needed so badly, she opened her laptop and slipped the virus disk, the small green floppy, into the drive. She clicked up Mozart's Ghost and, when the grinning guitar-playing skeleton appeared on her screen, she tapped her mouse on the concert information icon. The screen went blank and the little Greek pi sat blinking at the bottom of the blankness. Angela mouse-clicked on the pi, once again with dramatic results. The small screen went berserk as images erupted on it at lightning speed. Names, numbers, diagrams, and a recurrent letterhead – Atomic Energy Commission. Wow, this virus was taking her everywhere, even into highly-protected territory! Where was all this access coming from? Angela shook her head, baffled.

'Let's see if you've got a directory for this insanity,' she murmured out loud, typing in 'Dir'. Instantly, the screen froze, and a message scrolled in capital letters: INACCURATE COMMAND. KEY IN PASSWORD TO CONTINUE.

She needed an authorized password. Of course. But whose? Maybe Dale's. Angela thought for a moment, then she typed in 'Headbanger'.

At once the program went ballistic. A sharp alarm beep came out of the laptop, and a warning scrolled in bright red letters: UNAUTHORIZED ACCESS!! YOU ARE AN UNAUTHORIZED USER. FURTHER ATTEMPTS TO ACCESS WILL LEAD TO PROSECUTION!!

Whoa! Tough lockout! In computer parlance, Angela Bennett had just been 'flamed'.

Stunned, Angela quickly took her hands off the keyboard. 'Okay, okay,' she muttered. She backed off, closing out the program. The clock on the monitor read 11:02. She reached for the speed dial and punched in Cathedral Software, identifying herself and asking for Russ Melbourne, Dale Hessman's boss.

'Russ Melbourne here,' a man's voice said briskly. 'Angela! I thought you'd be long gone.'

'I was just about to leave, but – '

'Good, I'm glad you're still going,' Russ interrupted. 'But when you get back we need to talk. *Now* we're really desperately short of your genius up here.'

'Russ, believe me I'm no genius,' protested Angela, alarmed by the offer. She'd turned it down before, several times, but this time Russ sounded much more serious. 'Especially with an office full of people peering over my shoulder. Look, we've been over this before, and – '

'Just think about it in the next ten days, will you?' Russ pressed. 'The honchos up here aren't going to let me pick up someone new to replace Dale on such short notice, not with all the security breaches we've had in the past.'

'Replace Dale?' Angela Bennett's auburn brows darted up in surprise. 'Why? What happened?'

'Oh, God,' stammered Russ, stricken. 'I'm . . . I'm sorry. I thought you'd heard.'

'Heard what?' Chilly fingers grasped Angela Bennett's heart as she had a sudden premonition that Russ Melbourne might say something she didn't want to hear. And he said it. 'Angela, Dale's dead. His plane crashed last night outside L.A.'

The chill of the premonition turned to the ice of reality. She was too stunned to move or speak, and

34

only dimly did Angela Bennett hear Russ's voice coming out of the speaker, suddenly anxious. 'Angela?'

'My God!' Angela breathed at last. 'I . . . I just spoke to him yesterday. It can't be! He was coming down to see me.'

Now it was Russ's turn to fall silent. After a minute, he said softly, 'Kinda puts things in perspective, doesn't it. It's terrible.'

'Yeah, yeah,' Angela whispered shakily. Dale Hessman dead! She still couldn't take it all in. 'Look . . . I, uh, I gotta . . . hang up . . . gotta go, okay?' Then she asked, half-afraid to know, 'Russ, did he have any family?'

He sighed deeply. 'Wife, two little kids. One's the age of my Marny.'

A heavy weight settled over Angela's heart and tears welled up in her eyes. 'It's awful,' she whispered. 'Could you . . . ? I'd like to send them something.'

'Send it here, I'll make sure they get it,' Russ promised. 'Well, let's talk when you get back. And try to have a good vacation.'

Angela smiled bitterly. 'Yeah, thanks.'

Russ Melbourne could read the bitterness in her voice. 'Angela . . . there's nothing you can do,' he reassured her.

'I know, I know. G'bye, Russ.'

She ended the call and stood up, feeling stiff and shaky at the same time. She really did have to go if she wanted to make that flight. Russ was right; there was nothing she could do. A plane crash was a terrible thing, but at least it was an instant death, almost a merciful one. And an accident; who could predict an accident?

Automatically, without thinking, Angela began to tidy her desktop. She couldn't just go away leaving her office in disorder. She switched off her computers and covered the monitors and keyboards with plastic covers to keep the dust out. Her laptop she slipped into a small canvas case; she never went anywhere without it, not even on vacation to the Yucatan. Arranging her papers in a neat little stack, Angela picked up the loose diskettes lying on her desk, organizing them in her disk storage box, and laid the FedEx mailer from Cathedral Software on top. Poor Dale's 'weirdness' disk – they'd never talk about it now. Whatever virus Mozart's Ghost had caught, *she'd* never be curing it. It wasn't her business any more. Angela Bennett uttered a heavy sigh, then she hefted her laptop and brought it out to the car with her.

Angela parked her car in the long-term parking lot and made a note of the location, H4, on her parking ticket. It was twenty to twelve, and her flight must be boarding right now. She was going to be very late; she still had to get from the parking lot to the departure terminal. Panicking, clutching her carryon, her beach bag and her laptop, her backpack and shoulder purse bumping behind her, she raced toward the shuttle bus, which sat waiting with open doors at the edge of the lot.

36

'Plenty of time, sis,' the driver assured her, grinning. 'Plenty. Ain't nothing comin' or goin' in the friendly skies. They been flyin' around in circles for the past hour.'

He wasn't kidding. When they got to the terminal, Angela could see that LAX was a madhouse, sheer bedlam. Hundreds of people were milling around, angry, shrill, frightened, confused. Where were their gates? How were they supposed to get to their planes? Frustrated passengers were snapping at the reservations clerks, and the harassed airline personnel were growling right back at the customers.

Limo drivers were everywhere, clutching those crude little hand-printed signs they held up for incoming passengers, but there were no incoming passengers. They were still up there in the sky, circling Los Angeles Airport, not cleared to land. The tower's computers were going nuts. Relatives were looking for the gates to meet their loved ones, but the gates themselves were a total mystery. The computerized departure and arrival screens, usually models of correct advice for travellers, blinked madly with conflicting information. The same flights were listed as arriving, delayed, cancelled, crashed, hijacked, all at the same time, rendering the screens useless. Skycaps were trundling carts of luggage over protesting toes.

Angela turned pale and found it hard to draw a breath. This was her worst nightmare, pandemonium, a large crowd of angry people pushing and shoving everywhere she looked. She couldn't hack this, never!

For a minute, she cringed just inside the automatic doorway, unable to enter the airport, just watching and listening with a churning stomach.

'What's going on? What does that mean?' one irate woman was demanding, redfaced, as she pointed to the digital arrival screen, which kept on scrolling disinformation at warp speed. 'My daughter's on that flight!'

The flustered ticket agent was fielding a dozen questions from all sides at the same time. 'We don't know what it means ... I mean we know what it means, but – ' she stammered. There was no way she could explain this madness. The computers were not only down, they were going nuts.

Over the public address system a tape-recorded digitalized voice was repeating over and over, ' ... Cancelled due to mechanical problems, and we hope to have the situation corrected shortly ...'

One furious passenger had lost it, and had been making a noisy scene. Now he was being escorted out by a security guard, and he was yelling, 'I've got to get to Cleveland! Don't shove me, I've got rights, asshole!'

'We apologize for any inconvenience,' the mechanical voice droned through the overhead speakers.

What's going on? Angela wondered. She had been hugging the wall, watching the chaos. Now, slowly, reluctantly, she began to inch her way into the crowd, trying to get someone's attention, so that she could ask for an explanation. But nobody had a minute to spare for a shy girl with a soft voice and a puzzled face. Los Angeles Airport was one of the busiest airports in the country, and it had been stopped cold.

As though 'stopped cold' was their cure, at that very moment every computer screen blanked out, and the tape-recorded public announcement fell silent in mid-syllable.

'Ma'am, there's nothing I can do,' the flustered ticket clerk pleaded, but the angry woman wasn't about to accept that answer. She snarled, 'Well, god-damnit, somebody better do something –'

'It's those damn air traffic controllers out again,' one passenger growled, but a Skycap shook his head. 'No, man, I heard it's somethin' funky with the radar system. The whole airport's down.'

I can't do this, Angela thought. I can't. I've got to get out of here. But she remained in the airport, frozen to the spot. She couldn't bring herself to move. Too many noisy people were streaming past her with angry, scowling faces. It was getting harder for her even to draw a breath.

At last she spotted a few empty seats at the refreshment counter, and Angela slid gratefully into one of them, ordering a diet soda with lime. Above the counter, a TV monitor was broadcasting the CNN news. She kept one eye on the broadcast while she sipped her drink. Finishing the soda, she was too embarrassed to stay there without ordering, so she had another. The CNN anchor was sounding grave. On the screen behind him was a blownup visual of T. Michael Bergstrom.

' . . . And rumours abound in Washington political

circles,' he was saying, 'that a blood test taken last week at Bethesda Naval Hospital as part of his annual physical did in fact reveal that the Undersecretary of Defense, T. Michael Bergstrom, *was* infected with the AIDS virus. Bergstrom, well known for his opposition to gays serving in the military, is survived by his wife and young son ...'

Angela half-heard the newscast; the story meant nothing to her. One of the guys behind the counter came over to her.

'You okay?'

Did it show? Angela looked embarrassed; 'Yeah,' she mumbled. 'It's just that these crowds – '

'No, I mean are you okay with your soda?' He indicated her empty paper cup.

'Oh, no I'm fine. I've had three already. One more, and I'll probably fly myself to Mexico.'

'Looks like you won't have to,' he said, and pointed to the screens behind her. Angela turned.

Miraculously, as quickly as the craziness began, it was all over. Suddenly, the departure and arrival screens were blinking on, scrolling accurate gates and times. 'Thank you for your patience.' The public address system was working again, this time with a live human voice. 'The ... technical difficulty has been rectified. Please consult the arrival and departure boards for correct flight information ...'

The crowd stopped milling around and checked the monitors, moving off in a fairly orderly way towards their gates, either to meet planes or leave on them. Able to breathe again, Angela picked up her carryon bag and laptop computer, and joined the line at the escalator. But before she got up to the moving stairs, the crush proved too much for her, giving her that dreaded hemmed-in feeling, so she broke away and headed to an empty staircase. It was a tiring climb, followed by a long walk to her gate, but to Angela Bennett walking was greatly preferable to riding a crowded escalator. The bedlam at the airport had at least one upside – it had delayed her plane and she would make her flight after all.

This was off-season; the Krystal resort hotel was half-empty and the beach uncrowded, exactly as Angela had hoped. Even so, there were more tourists in Yucatan than she was comfortable with. She took herself off to the ocean, finding the least populated part of the beach. Here, at last Angela allowed herself to relax, to enjoy the warmth, the ocean, the lush vegetation, the soft, lapping sound of the waves, the fresh sea air, the little thatched native huts that so picturesquely ringed the pale sands of the beach. Here she had found both sunlight and privacy – nobody in the Yucatan was interested in Angela Bennett, and she couldn't ask for anything better than that. In the six days since she'd arrived, the only conversations she had held were with the desk clerk, when she'd dropped off or picked up her room key, with the maid who came to make up the room, and with the waiters who scurried around the beach taking drink orders. And those conversations comprised only four or five necessary words, mostly *por favor, gracias, de nada*.

She spent most of her time lying on a hotel towel at the beach, her eyes hidden behind large sunglasses. Sometimes she read a page or two of the paperback novel she'd brought with her. More often she just dozed lightly, enjoying the sun and the sand and the sea, while the neglected novel lay face-down on the beach. Angela had built a little fortress around herself, without even realizing it. Her large beach bag, her laptop case, a bunch of magazines – these were piled around her like the crenellated parapet on a fortified castle. They said clearly, 'Go away. I'd rather be alone.'

Now, with her vacation just about over and a flight home scheduled for the next day, Angela had managed to relax at last. This week-long holiday had been very good for her; her mother's illness, Venice, Cathedral, the sudden death of Dale Hessman – all seemed far away and nothing that she had to deal with. For six days she had slept a lot, soundly and dreamlessly. But now she was suddenly wide awake; that last nap had refreshed her. Angela sat up, a little bored. For six days she hadn't touched her computer, but now she was in the mood for playing one of the game disks she'd brought with her. Reaching over, she grabbed her laptop and pulled it towards her, opening the cover and switching it on. Now she was an Internaut again, travelling through cyberspace.

But instead of the opening menu she expected, Angela saw a familiar skeleton and these words on the screen: 'Mozart's Ghost Web Server. For the Ultimate Enthusiast.'

What the hell? Immediately, Angela realized what had happened. She hadn't emptied the disk drive when she left home; Dale's green disk was still in it. Angela was sure she'd put in back in the FedEx envelope on her desk, but here it was in her laptop. She reached around and popped the disk out of the drive. Dale's handwriting all over it; it gave her goose bumps. But sick or well, Mozart's Ghost had nothing to do with her anymore, so she tossed the disk into her beach bag and fished out Enyggma, a challenging computer game. Putting the diskette in the A drive, she booted up and began to play, reaching Level Three in under four minutes.

Concentrating on the game, she didn't even see the waiter or the person next to her on the beach who had summoned him. The first thing that caught her attention was the hotel guest saying, 'Gibson, please.' Evidently the waiter had no idea of what a Gibson was, because the man added, 'It's a Martini with an onion instead of an olive.'

Just hearing the word Gibson, Angela found that she was ragingly thirsty. The thought of an icy cold Gibson, the sweet, salty taste of the pickled onion, the sharpness of the gin, made her really crave one. 'Could you make me one, too, please?' she asked the waiter.

The man on the beach shot a look at her. Self-conscious, as always, Angela turned her eyes away, although not before noting that the man in modest

43

black swim trunks was fairly young, probably middle to late thirties, slim build but nicely smooth-muscled, dark hair, pleasant face, not strikingly handsome yet easy to look at. She also noticed that the man seemed to be getting ready to leave the beach; he had already folding his towel and was packing up a book and a water bottle.

'I'll take mine up at the bar,' he told the waiter, putting his sunblock into his gym bag. Then, as the waiter left to put in the drink order at the bar, the man remarked, 'I didn't think anybody else drank those any more.' His words held just a touch of a charming British accent.

Angela looked up, a little startled. Was he talking to her? Evidently he was, but it was an innocuous comment, and it wouldn't kill her to be polite.

'Me neither,' she said. 'I guess I'm not that un-fashionable after all.'

Standing up, the man began to walk away. But when he saw her laptop, he stopped in his tracks. 'Hmmm, business or pleasure?'

Angela's face turned red; she was embarrassed to be caught playing a computer game like a teenager. She hit Escape and the screen went blank. 'There's a difference?' she said.

The man grinned – he had a killer smile – and dug into his gym bag, pulling out a laptop computer that was the same make and model as Angela's. 'If you're a hacker, not a whole lot.'

At the sight of the small computer, Angela relaxed a little. Here was somebody who understood. 'Nice

piece of hardware. You in the racket, too?' she asked
lightly.

'You know anybody who isn't?' he countered.

Bullseye. Angela smiled back, unaware of how
pretty a picture she was making at that moment.
'Nope.' She shook her head.

'Are we pathetic or what?' The dark-haired man
shook his head, too. 'Here we are on the most perfect
beach in the world and all we can think of is – '

'Where the hell can I hook up my modem?' finished
Angela, and the two of them burst into shared
laughter. They'd made a connection. Two of a kind.
Kindred spirits. Computer geeks. He held out his
hand. 'Jack Devlin.'

She shook his hand with shy pleasure. 'Angela Bennett.'

'Angela Bennett, throw your things into your bag.
C'mon, have your Gibson up on the veranda, with
me.'

How could she refuse? More to the point, *why*
should she refuse? Angela felt a little nervous as she
stood up, self-consciously aware that she was wearing
only a skimpy bathing suit. She was aware, too, of the
magnetism and good looks of Jack Devlin. Physically,
he was very much her type. She wasn't into macho
men, men whose neck measurements were larger than
their IQs. Even so, as attracted as she was to him,
Angela was glad she was going home tomorrow. A
vacation romance wasn't for her. She was too vulnerable, too shy to open herself up on short-term
acquaintance. But just a drink, why not? What harm
could come of having a drink with an attractive man?

45

One drink turned into two, two into three. By the time the waiter took away the empties and set the fourth pair of Gibsons, sweating in chilled glasses, down in front of them, Angela was feeling no pain. For two hours she and Devlin had been sitting in the refreshing shade of this bamboo and palm veranda, inhaling the sweet, intoxicating fragrance of the bougainvillea vines blossoming over the roof, just perched here quietly, drinking and talking.

Sitting here talking with Jack Devlin was one of the greatest pleasures Angela had ever experienced. Their conversation ranged over a hundred topics, serious and trivial alike. He was smart, he was funny, he was outgoing, and it didn't hurt that he had those devastating Black Irish looks – cleft in his chin, jet black hair and bright brown eyes. How could she have ever have thought he wasn't handsome? Devlin was gorgeous, especially when he flashed that grin, which he seemed to be doing all the time.

And everything he said rang a bell with Angela. Never had she met anybody who seemed to be fixed so firmly on her wavelength, who brought out the humour in her, whose sensitivity made her feel so comfortable. They'd known each other only two hours, yet she felt that she'd been acquainted with Jack Devlin all her life – or was it the powerful icy gin that gave her that impression?

Whatever caused this mellow feeling, Angela enjoyed it. She'd opened up to Jack like a flower to the sun; she couldn't remember a time when she'd laughed so much. They'd been comparing notes on their lives, finding much in common. He was treating her like an attractive woman, but at the same time as an equal.

'Okay,' she laughed. 'I told you, now it's your turn.'

Devlin shook his head, grinning. 'Naw, it's okay. Let's move on.'

Angela wasn't about to accept this. 'Hey, not fair! I showed you mine, you have to show me yours.'

This made Jack Devlin laugh out loud. 'Wishing you could be invisible as a kid does not constitute an "embarrassing" secret,' he protested. But Angela was giving him such a pleading look that he gave in. 'Okay, okay, my most embarrassing secret. Let me think . . . you know "Breakfast at Tiffany's"?'

Angela beamed at him tipsily. 'You kidding? My favourite movie . . . I just about wore out my credit card renting it.'

Devlin nodded solemnly. 'Okay, then you'll know what I'm talking about here. I had this sort of identity crisis when I was thirteen . . . Christ, this is mortifying . . . I used to think I was one of the characters.'

'Audrey Hepburn?' laughed Angela.

'Not *that* mortifying. No, the cat.'

Angela almost choked on her cocktail onion. 'The *cat*?'

He nodded his head. 'The cat. And I'd play out that last scene of the movie about five hundred times a day. There I am in that alleyway, in the pouring rain, scared to death, soaked to the bone, totally aban-doned – '

Angela had always wept shamelessly at that final scene. Tears stung her eyelids now as she remembered that poor red cat, thrown out into the outside world by Holly Golightly in her denial of commitment. If the drenched ginger cat hadn't been rescued at the eleventh hour by Audrey Hepburn and George Peppard, she would never have been able to sit through the film. And to think that this intelligent man was sensitive enough to understand and empathize? She couldn't believe this guy! Talk about too good to be true . . .

They fell silent, wordlessly sharing the poignant moment. Angela felt an emotional bond forming with this stranger, and it scared her. Suddenly Devlin threw back his head and began to croon offkey. 'Moooon Riverrrrrr. . . . wiiider than a millllle. . . .' Angela joined in, and they broke up laughing at how rotten they were. The potential intimacy of the moment dissipated into laughter.

Devlin leaned across the table toward Angela, appreciating her glow, the softness of her large eyes, the sweet sunny smell of her skin. 'Would you have dinner . . . I mean with me . . . tonight?' he asked her softly.

Angela gnawed at her lip, a sure sign of indecisiveness with her. She was tempted; she really did want to have dinner with Jack Devlin, and have this special day not come to an end, but . . . 'Thanks, but I really can't,' she said. 'I've got an early flight home, and – '

'You sure?' Devlin asked, looking into her face.

48

'Your last night?' His dark eyes were mesmerizing, and he was altogether so appealing that a dazzled Angela had to catch her breath.

'You know, I'd love to, but –' She decided to come clean; he deserved her total honesty. 'I just can't deal with the hotel dining room. I've had almost every meal in my room,' she confessed, her cheeks turning a dull red. Her fear of the stifling presence of other people was truly the most embarrassing secret of Angela Bennett's life.

'Problem solved,' Devlin said lightly. 'There's this place out on the little island of Cozumel, just off the tip of the peninsula, in the Gulf, and what they can do with a roast pig is downright delicious. Tourists can't be bothered. It's too far off the beaten track. You can't even get there by car. You'll see. It'll be just you, me and half a dozen bored-out-of-their-skulls waiters. What do you say?'

What could she say? The combination of the hot sun and the cool Gibsons and Jack Devlin's beautiful dark eyes and his offer of a delicious dinner in an un-crowded place with the most attractive, sensitive man she'd ever met – it was all too much for Angela. She gave in with a smile.

'All right, deal. But just one thing. If it's so secluded you can't get there by car, how do we get there?'

Devlin grinned that killer grin, and his eyes sparkled. 'You'll find out,' he promised. 'Now go get dressed and meet me down there in an hour.' He pointed down the beach to a wooden pier jutting out into the water.

Angela showered and dressed quickly, then undressed again and threw everything out of the closet and the drawers on to the bed. Damn it, why didn't she own anything halfway decent to wear? Why hadn't she gone shopping for a few nice things before she left Venice? After dithering over her few garments, she settled on a blouse and a side-wrapped skirt. Sitting down at the dressing table, Angela Bennett pulled her dark red hair back off her face, exposing her remarkable cheekbones and her wide forehead, large eyes, perfectly-shaped lips, cleft chin, straight nose, and feathery eyebrows. She stared at her reflection in the mirror, unsatisfied, her insecurities making her unable to recognize just how attractive she really was. Well, this is my face, take it or leave it. Not a lot I can do about it now.

She stood up to go, but self-consciousness held her back. Pulling her blouse out of the waistband of her skirt, Angela knotted it into a kind of midriff and checked the effect in the mirror. Better? Not as good? But she couldn't decide. She took a glance at her watch. Oh, God, she was already late. Angela snatched up her beach bag and tossed everything out of it into her purse. Passport, credit cards, travellers cheques, cash, even Dale's disk – all tumbled into one compartment of her purse. Then she dashed out of her hotel room and ran down along the beach to the jetty.

Jack Devlin was already there waiting for her, his dark hair attractively ruffled by the evening wind. In a white linen jacket and open-collared black shirt he was even more gorgeous than Angela remembered. And just as gorgeous was the long, sleek cabin cruiser moored at the jetty, with 'Innovative' painted on its stern. The beautiful cruiser was so large it even had its own outboard dinghy, attached by a rope behind.

'We're going in *this*,' squeaked Angela in disbelief.

'Company perk,' smiled Devlin.

'Some perk,' Angela smiled back. 'Some company. I think that one year I got a calendar from Cathedral.'

Angela didn't know much about boats, but as they boarded she looked around in something very like awe. This was obviously the top of the line in its class, with every bell and whistle a cabin cruiser could cram on to its teak decks. The boat virtually glistened with newness and glamour, from its sleek hull to its multi-bank control console. They were alone, she was happy to note, no crew would be needed tonight with this cruiser that practically sailed itself.

They went down into the small neat cabin. Devlin rummaged under the counter and came up with a handful of CDs. 'Hope you're crazy for Motown,' he smiled.

'Only slightly less insane than I am about Otis Redding,' replied Angela.

Jack's smile widened to an Irish grin as he pulled out a handful of CDs and got the music going.

The start of a perfect evening, up on deck in the Gulf of Mexico, cutting through the water at high speed, the warm gulf spray drenching Angela's hair and skin and clothing as the smoky dusk enveloped her, and she and Jack Devlin yowling 'Knock on

51

Wood' at the top of their powerful lungs as they laughed and kicked their feet and pounded the deck in time to the song. Angela was having a wonderful time, and the best part of it was the serendipity, the complete unexpectedness of the encounter. Who would have thought that Angela Bennett would meet such a great guy on the last night of her vacation?

Dinner was everything that Jack Devlin had promised. The food was wonderful, the roast pig crisp and savoury, the baked plantains mealy and sweet, the beans fiery with chilli peppers, the tortillas soft and piping hot, the Dos Equis beer cold and tangy enough. They were the only guests in the place, which was little more than an island hut, tin-roofed as most small structures were on Cozumel, but with a grass-roofed veranda where they were sitting and en-joying the evening. Beyond the restaurant, they could see a forest of brush and palm trees with thick branching trunks covered in flowering vines. Above them, a giant tropical moon shone over the Gulf; the heavens were lit up by bright constellations. Around them, smiling waiters piled their plates high and re-freshed their drinks and spoke no English.

A Mexican woman with a Polaroid camera came over to their table and snapped their picture, and Jack gave her a handful of pesetas for the print of the two of them smiling, Jack and Angela, heads nearly touch-ing, the print which he tucked away into his shirt pocket. Souvenir.

'So?' Jack turned back to Angela, who during the meal had been opening up to him, beginning to tell him the truth about herself. He listened with interest to her explanation, and his expression was a cross between sympathy and amusement.

'So ... it's not really like claustrophobia, not really agoraphobia ... it's more a choice I've made,' she said slowly. 'I just don't want a lot of people around me. There aren't many crowds where I come from.'

Jack playfully turned his ear towards her. 'And that'd be, if my ears don't deceive me ... Colorado? Eastern ... no, southeastern part of the state.'

Angela sat back in her chair, astonished and impressed. Was there no limit to this man's interesting facets? The teeming metropolis of La Junta,' she admitted. 'Population fifty. Is it that strong after all these years?'

Devlin shrugged. 'No, it's a trick I do,' he said lightly. 'Why "after all these years"? When did you leave?'

'Like a lifetime ago. I was fifteen going on ten. We moved to Denver, Phoenix, Tulsa, San Jose – '

Jack nodded, smiling gently. 'Father got transferred a lot,' he suggested.

A shadow passed across Angela's lovely face. 'No ... he just ... transferred out ... for good one day. And since La Junta's not exactly the employment capital of the world, Mom chased after jobs, and chased and chased.'

Jack Devlin looked across the table sympathetically. 'I was a diplomat's kid, always on the move. I know what it was like, never fitting in – '

Angela nodded her head in vigorous agreement.

'You end up being the "new kid" so many times, you give up trying to make friends – '

' – Feeling like the biggest square peg in recorded history – ' finished Jack. 'And then along came computers. Computers are your life, aren't they?'

'Yes. The perfect hiding place,' beamed Angela, then she broke off red-faced as she felt rather than saw Jack's eyes, suddenly serious, bent on her. 'What are you looking at?'

'Your face,' he said softly. 'How it goes to neon when we talk computers.'

Angela's blush deepened, and she turned her face away from his probing glance and his melting smile. 'I've got one or two other interests, you know.'

'Oh, yes? Such as?' he mocked gently, with a sceptical lift of his brow. 'So tell me, what's your speciality?'

'Almost everything. Beta testing, mainly.'

Jack whistled. 'Miles out of my league,' he told her admiringly.

Angela laughed deprecatingly. 'Not quite. It boils down to glorified troubleshooting of programs a ten-year-old could design. All I do is access people's systems, find their faults and fix them.'

'What if they don't have any faults?' he asked.

Angela looked at him, amused. 'I've yet to meet a system that didn't have faults.'

'And you find them all.'

'I try.'

'I'll bet you're good at it,' he grinned charmingly. 'Too damn good. I wouldn't want you to go looking for *my* faults, Angela.'

'Don't worry,' she smiled back at him. 'I won't.' Right now, she couldn't imagine what faults Jack Devlin might have, and she didn't give a damn. She was making every effort to forget herself and enjoy the moment, to push the thought of going back tomorrow out of her mind.

Dinner over at last, they strolled side by side down the beach toward the rickety pier where the cabin cruiser was anchored. Ringing the beach was thick tropical vegetation, filled with shadows. High clouds were drifting across the moon, and a stiff evening breeze was blowing up. Angela shivered and wrapped her arms around herself, over her bare midriff which was developing gooseflesh.

'Cold?' asked Jack.

'Not really,' she lied. She didn't want this moment to come to an end just because she was feeling a little chilly.

But Devlin didn't want the moment to end, either. He took a large silk handkerchief from his jacket and, getting down on his knees, he wrapped it around Angela's body, taking his time, knotting it behind her. For a moment he knelt there before her, his arms around her body, while Angela trembled a little, entranced by the kind of thoughtful gesture she'd dreamed of so often but had never experienced. This exceptional man was making her feel like a princess. 'Thank you,' she whispered.

It was the perfect moment for them to kiss; their faces were only inches apart. Angela closed her eyes. Her lips were already tingling expectantly.

But Jack didn't kiss her; instead, he pulled away from her, his face unreadable. He took a pack of cigarettes – Newports – out of his pocket. Lighting one, he dragged on it deeply, then he continued walking down the beach with Angela beside him. She felt a pang of disappointment.

'I used to smoke those,' remarked Angela. 'Newports was my brand, too.'

'But you quit?' She nodded. 'Really? I refuse to quit,' Devlin continued. 'I figure you've got to work a few things in life without a net, or how are you going to know you're alive?'

'Hey, I take my share of risks!' Angela protested defensively. 'I don't always floss, sometimes I even rip the tags off my pillows.'

'What do you know, my kind of woman,' smiled Jack.

He was irresistible; Angela returned his smile. With every moment they spent together she was becoming more and more captivated by this man's powerful charm.

'Feeling adventurous?' he challenged.

Angela tilted her head to glance up at him. 'What do you have in mind?'

He held the Newport out to her. 'Dare you risk it?'

'How else do you know you're alive?' she laughed. They stopped, facing each other. Jack Devlin held the cigarette to Angela's lips, placing his other hand lightly on her back. Tentatively, shyly, she leaned into him a little. She was enmeshed in the moonlight and the spell of the tropics, the smell of tobacco and

56

tweed. Angela drew in her breath. A moment was definitely about to happen. This time they were going to kiss; she was certain of it.

Suddenly, out of the shadows of the palm trees behind them, a small figure darted out and grabbed Angela's bag, wrenching it from her shoulder and running back into the thick vegetation. The thief was no taller than a ten-year-old boy.

'Hey!' yelled Angela.

'Damn kids!' snarled Devlin, taking off after the purse snatcher. Angela chased after him.

'Jack! It's not worth getting killed over . . . please?' As the two figures disappeared into the tropical jungle, Angela stopped running, uncertain. She didn't know what to do, follow him or not? No, better stay here where he could find her again. They musn't be separated. All her thoughts were frantically bent on Jack Devlin; what if the thief had a knife or a gun? Oh, God, don't let anything happen to him! she begged silently, fearfully.

Jack Devlin pushed his way through the vegetation, searching for the purse snatcher. He stopped, listening carefully; he had lost sight of the small figure, but he could hear the crackling of branches nearby.

The thief ducked down behind a large sheltering tree. He was panting heavily and sweat was dripping down his small face. He started to move out of the shadows, when Devlin's hand grabbed him and whirled him around. The thief was not a boy at all, but a middle-aged man, tiny, wizened, wide-eyed as Jack Devlin held onto him tightly.

'Give that to me,' snarled Devlin.

The thief put Angela's purse into Jack's hand. Squatting on the ground, Devlin dumped the contents of the bag on to the earth, and roughly pawed through them. He pushed Angela's room key aside, paid no attention to her passport or credit cards. 'It's not here!' he growled angrily.

'It no in hotel,' said the thief, looking nervous. 'I look everywhere. So I come here, do like you say — whoosh! Like magician!'

'Yeah, you're the midget Houdini,' Devlin threw at him sourly, still searching. And then, 'Bingo!' he held it up triumphantly – Dale Hessman's virus disk.

The little man smiled, not a pretty sight. He put out a tiny, grimy hand. *'Bueno*. Okay, okay, *dinero, dinero.'*

Devlin nodded, and reached into his pocket. But what he held in his hand when he took it out was not the thief's expected payoff, but a payoff of a different kind. A 9mm pistol, its barrel elongated by an evil-looking silencer. Without changing expression, still on his knees, Jack Devlin pumped three bullets in rapid succession into the little man's head and chest, killing him instantly and without a sound. The thief fell dead at his knees. Devlin pushed him roughly to one side so that he could scoop up the rest of Angela's possessions, and stuff them into his pockets along with the disk.

'Jack? Jack!' called Angela from the beach, on a note of rising hysteria.

Devlin stood up. He grabbed up Angela's purse and

flung it far away, into a clump of trees. Then he mussed up his hair and rubbed dirt on his face and his shirt. Drawing a clasp knife from his pocket, he ran the sharp blade without hesitation over his left palm, making a shallow but bloody gash. Clutching his left hand in his right, he ran back in the direction of the beach.

3

When Angela saw Jack Devlin emerging from the bushes, panting and swearing under his breath, she raced to him. Never had she been so happy to see another human being.

'Sorry, he got away,' Devlin breathed heavily. 'So much for heroism.'

'It's okay, it's okay,' she assured him. But now that he was safe and sound in front of her eyes, Angela allowed herself to think of her stolen property. The enormity of it hit her all at once, and she gasped out, 'Oh, my God! My passport, my credit cards, everything!'

'C'mon,' said Devlin. 'There's a ship-to-shore on the boat. We can at least call in your credit cards.' He put his left hand on her arm.

Angela's eyes widened as for the first time she noticed his bleeding palm. He was wounded! 'My God! What happened? Are you okay?' she gasped.

'He had a knife. No big deal.' With a wry smile Devlin shrugged off her concern.

'Do you have first aid on the boat?'

'We have everything. My perk, remember?'

The *Innovative* was indeed well equipped; with the

contents of a large first aid box, Angela soon had Jack Devlin's wound cleaned and bandaged. 'You're bleeding to death and I'm whining about my MasterCard,' she told him ruefully, as she wound the gauze around his palm a few extra times. 'Shoot me, I'm an utter jerk.'

Devlin shook his head wryly. 'I'm the jerk, trying to impress you by – '

'For the future,' Angela interrupted, 'just know that the living tend to interest me just a little more than the dead do.' The bandage was nice and tight and couldn't use an inch more wrapping, but Angela wouldn't stop. She was reluctant to let go of Jack's hand.

'Now, that's a healthy sign,' Devlin grinned, his old charming self again. 'Come on, let's see if we can raise the Cozumel police on the ship-to-shore.'

But the radio wouldn't co-operate; all he was able to raise was a lot of static. 'It's not working. We need to head farther out,' explained Devlin as he fiddled with the dials. 'Terrain interference or something.'

But Angela had lost interest in the ship-to-shore. She was standing dreamily at the starboard rail of the *Innovative*, her hair blowing in the sea breeze, her smooth profile turned up to the heavens, warmed by the moonlight and the blanket of stars. Even with what had happened on the island, she had never felt quite so at ease with herself, or so peaceful. 'Take us to Morocco if you want,' she murmured happily. 'It's so beautiful out here.'

Devlin watched her for a moment, as Angela

moved gracefully aft to the stern, then he went into the cabin. His expression was inscrutable, but there was nothing left of Irish charm in it. Switching on the ignition, he turned the wheel, bringing the boat away from the dock and out to sea. The sleek hull travelled swiftly but smoothly through the Gulf waters.

To Angela the night was suffused with magic. The sea, the moon, the starlight, the presence of the man in the cabin, all spoke to her inner self with soothing words. The effect of the drinks she'd had before and during dinner had just about worn off, and the glow she was experiencing now had little or nothing to do with alcohol. Even the trauma of being robbed of her credit cards, passport and money – everything she needed to function in the real world – couldn't really darken her mood. Credit cards and passports can be replaced; the lost cash was negligible, only a few hundred dollars. The most important thing was that Jack Devlin hadn't been seriously hurt, and he was here, alone with her on this magnificent boat on this magnificent evening. Sure, he hadn't kissed her yet, but there had been two near misses, and Angela still had her hopes. She loved watching him at the helm controls, he seemed so in command.

They'd been heading out across the Gulf for about fifteen minutes, when Angela called out, 'How are we doing?' By now, she reckoned, there ought to be some clear transmission on the ship-to-shore.

'Still no dice,' Devlin called back. 'I'm just going below. Won't be a minute.' He went down into the bridge cabin, but he was nowhere near the radio, and he certainly had no intention of making contact with police. Moving to the computer console, he switched off the ignition, killing the engine dead. The *Innovative* floated silently on the Gulf Stream waters. Opening a drawer under the counter, Devlin chucked in the ignition keys, followed by the green Mozart's Ghost disk. Before closing the drawer, he pulled out of it a fully loaded 9mm ammunition clip. He removed the half-empty clip from his pistol and snapped in the full magazine, ramming it home with a satisfying click. Then, silently, Jack Devlin let Angela Bennett's house and car keys and identification documents – her credit cards, her driver's licence, her passport – slip overboard into the inky waters of the Gulf of Mexico. One credit card, Angela's Visa, he kept ... just in case. This one he thrust into his trouser pocket.

For a long moment, Jack Devlin watched Angela Bennett's precious proofs of identity sink beneath the surface. She wouldn't be needing them any more, not ever again.

Then he put the fully loaded gun into his right-hand jacket pocket, keeping his hand curled around the butt, and emerged on deck, walking toward the stern where Angela was waiting, gazing out at the sea.

'Maybe we're still not far enough out?' she called to the cabin.

'No,' he said evenly. 'This should do it.'

Angela turned. Just the sight of Jack Devlin made her happy. As soon as she saw him her face lit up with her beautiful bright smile. They were now no more than two feet apart; even through the salt in the air she could smell the tobacco of the cigarettes Jack smoked. Her eyes looked deeply into his trying to read his thoughts.

If she only could have read his thoughts . . .

Jack Devlin began to pull his right hand from his jacket pocket, the hand closing tightly around the powerful silenced pistol. But before he could complete the act, his arms were being pinned tightly to his sides in a strong, warm embrace. Angela was pressing up against him, whispering in his ear, 'Tonight's been so out of control – ' And, before he could say or do anything, her full red lips were pressed tightly to his in a deep, passionate kiss.

Devlin's eyes opened wide in surprise, then, even more to his surprise, he found himself returning the kiss just as passionately, his arms pulling Angela even closer to him, his body responding to the fire in hers. Devlin made no effort to stop her when her hands ran up his chest under his jacket, and when she pushed it off his shoulders, he helped her. Slipping his arms out of the sleeves, he threw it to the deck. There was a small thump, the sound of a heavy gun muffled by layers of linen. Devlin was aware of it, but Angela heard nothing but the thumping of the blood in her veins.

Later, after they had made long, satisfying love, they lay side by side on deck cushions, covered by a canvas tarpaulin, staring up at the stars. Around them, their clothes were scattered in the carelessness of sudden heat. And, of course, after all that unexpected intimacy, Angela was experiencing the insecurity and remorse that seemed to dog her heels throughout her life. 'You know. . . . I hope you don't take this the wrong way . . . but this is not my style . . .'

'And I thought you took risks,' grinned Devlin.

'No . . .' Angela explained uncomfortably, embarrassed. 'I mean . . . I don't know . . . first-date sex, one night stand . . . it's really not me . . . maybe I'll just shut up now.'

'You've always been a relationship kind of girl,' Devlin murmured as he stroked Angela's bare shoulders.

'Absolutely. Both times,' she answered seriously.

He couldn't help it; Jack Devlin threw his head back in a yelp of laughter. He should have known. Only two lovers in how many? . . . twenty-five years? Sitting up on his elbow, he turned his face to Angela. 'How long has it been since the last relationship?'

'1993.' She gave a wry shake of her auburn head.

'Let's see,' he guessed, teasing. 'Who was he? College boyfriend? I bet he was the captain of the drinking team, wasn't ready for a "relationship" . . .'

'I should be so lucky.' Angela smiled ruefully. 'My shrink, actually. You know the story . . . I thought I was lonely . . . he forgot he was married . . . it didn't last very long.' Her expressive face looked suddenly sad as bitter memories flooded back. 'My mom was diagnosed with Alzheimer's around the same time and – you don't want to hear this – you know, I think I'm gonna shut up right now, and just be quiet.'

'It's okay,' Devlin smiled.

'Well, *I* don't want to hear it,' Angela said. 'I'm sorry. I'm rambling. I'm just a little nervous, I guess.'

'Nothing to be nervous about,' Devlin replied, suddenly expressionless. 'You want a drink?'

'That'd be greatly appreciated,' Angela breathed gratefully. She shivered a little with the cold. 'Thank you.'

Jack Devlin pulled his pants and shirt on and went into the bridge cabin. If anybody needed a drink, he did. He was furious with himself for having allowed this to get out of hand and go so far. Sure, Angela Bennett was attractive ... damned attractive ... but that was definitely beside the point. He couldn't afford to allow himself to be sucked in, or to feel anything for her. The beautiful, sweet Angela Bennett was dead meat, on the way out. It was time to put a clean end to this business, more than time.

Devlin stared for a minute at the souvenir Polaroid photo of the two of them that was propped up near the wheel, on the control panel. Then he grabbed a bottle of wine, opened it quickly, poured some into a glass and downed it in a gulp. That's better. Now he filled a glass for Angela.

Out on deck the night air was getting even colder. Angela pulled her clothing on, but it was only a thin blouse and skirt and was still more than a little damp from the spray. Jack Devlin's linen jacket beckoned to her. Grabbing it up, she shrugged into it and pulled it around her. Then, to warm her hands, she plunged them into the pockets.

Devlin came out on deck carrying the wine bottle and

two stemmed glasses. When he saw her, he stopped short.

Angela Bennett was sitting on deck, smoking one of Devlin's Newports. On her lap was his 9mm pistol.

'What's this for?' she asked quietly.

Damn! Mustn't spook her, thought Jack Devlin. Out loud, he said lightly, 'Just another perk. For shark fishing. Careful with that –'

'Shark fishing with a silencer?'

Carefully, Devlin set down the bottle and the glasses. He reached out casually for his gun, but Angela's reaction was to tighten her hand over it, holding it. 'You certainly know your ordnance,' he told her.

'Colorado,' shrugged Angela, expressionless. 'You grow up with guns.'

Jack Devlin smiled, a wide smile, a disarming smile, a 'trust-me, baby' smile. Angela raised her hand from the gun. Devlin reached over and lifted it from her lap, then slowly took two steps back.

'So, who are you, Jack?' she asked him nervously.

Devlin turned to her, his face drawn into a bitter mask. 'Who am I?' he snarled. 'I'll tell you who I am. Captain Goddamn America meets Albert Schweitzer, isn't that what you wanted?' He flung his words at her mockingly. 'Oh, yes, I remember now. "Butch, beautiful, brilliant, spends all day dashing into the fray, fists flying –" Sorry, I don't know any organ cantatas.'

With horror, Angela recognized her own words from the Cyber Chat bulletin board. How did he know? Had he been listening in? For how long? And why? Suddenly she felt as though she'd been raped. If Jack Devlin had physically forced himself on her, he could not have violated her more hideously or more painfully. Incredulous, she stared at him.

'And, if you'll excuse me,' he said coldly as he raised the gun to her head, 'it's time to make the world safe for democracy.' In the split second before the long pistol barrel touched her head, Angela screamed out, 'Jesus! No!'

Without another word Jack Devlin pulled the trigger, once, twice, three times.

The gun clicked every time, but it didn't fire. Devlin stared at the empty pistol in his hand, then at the cowering Angela. 'Where's the clip?' he demanded coldly.

Nearly paralyzed with fear, Angela held up the ammunition magazine. As Devlin made a dive for it, she moved quickly, throwing it overboard. Savagely, he lunged at her, but she scrambled backward across the deck, never taking her eyes off him. She was still hanging on to the lit cigarette. 'Why?! Why me?' she screamed.

Jack Devlin had no time for words. This was killing time. He had a job to do. He flung his body on top of her, his hands reaching for and finding Angela's throat. He began to squeeze, powerful fingers wrapped around her windpipe. Angela struggled wildly, her arms flailing, but Jack Devlin was too strong for her. She felt the air being compressed from her lungs, the life being squeezed out of her. She

68

couldn't draw in a breath, and was starting to black out.

Still choking and gasping, with a desperate movement of her hand Angela drove the burning end of her cigarette into Devlin's eye. He shrieked loudly in his agony, and his hands fell away from her throat, clutching at his eye.

Angela rolled to one side, frantically searching for a weapon, any weapon she could find. Her scrabbling hand touched the wine bottle, and she grabbed it. She raised it and swung it hard at Devlin's head. The bottle smashed and he went down hard, like a felled tree. He uttered one loud groan, his head hit the deck railing, and was out cold.

For a long moment Angela stood over him, the broken bottle jagged edge out, poised to strike him again if necessary. But Devlin was lying very still. Was he breathing? It was almost impossible to tell. Could he be dead? Shivering, she threw the bottle as far away from her as she could. It tumbled end over end overboard. She rushed back to where Devlin was lying, knelt at his side and began to rummage through his clothes. The answer must be there somewhere, in his jacket, or maybe in his trouser pockets. But all she came up with was a wallet. She had to find some help.

Clutching Devlin's wallet tightly, she raced into the cabin, and frantically spun the dial of the ship-to-shore. 'I need help! Can anyone hear me? Emergency! Help, please!' But all she got was static; she flipped switches, more static. Damn! This wasn't working. Angela gave it up; instead she rifled through the contents of the wallet under the light of the control panel.

A thick sheaf of bills, most of them in hundred-dollar denominations; some Mexican currency; but no form of identification – no credit cards, no driver's licence. Nothing that explained to Angela why the hell this man was trying to blow her away.

Angela shoved the wallet back into the jacket pocket and moved to the helm. But the wheel wouldn't move; there was no key in the ignition. Where the hell was the damn key? If she couldn't get the boat started, she'd be stuck out here in the middle of the Gulf of Mexico, with a corpse or ... if Devlin wasn't dead ... with a man whose only intention was to make her dead. She had to find those keys! Angela turned to the drawers in the console, pulling them out one after another, emptying them in her desperate search for the keys to the boat.

Yes! Here were keys and ... Dale's disk. The Mozart's Ghost virus disk. Without stopping to reason it out, Angela instinctively made the connection between the virus disk and what was happening tonight. This was what he wanted! This damn virus was probably why she had nearly lost her life. Why she was still in danger. *Can't think about that now* ... Angela shoved the disk deep into her pocket next to Devlin's wallet. She turned to the ignition, fitting the key in. At first it seemed to work. The motor started smoothly, but the boat still didn't move.

What was she supposed to do now? Angela hadn't the foggiest idea of how to drive this criminally expensive state-of-the-art tugboat; it wasn't anything like driving a car. The numbers on the dials, the depth gauges and other controls – she didn't know how to read them or even what they were. She glanced nervously over her shoulder to check if Devlin was still unconscious, but she couldn't see him from where she was. Angela turned back to the helm, determined to get this vessel underway fast. She grabbed at the gear shift, yanking hard on the handle. There was an awful grinding as the gears clashed, but the boat stayed put. Suddenly, without warning, the motor stopped dead.

'Shit!' yelled Angela, scared, angry, frustrated, as she pounded her fists on the wheel. 'Shit! Shit!'

Wait a minute! Wasn't there a dinghy back there, tied to the stern? She'd almost forgotten. Tearing out of the cabin, Angela hurled the boat keys into the ocean. She raced to the stern, past Devlin's still-unconscious body, and climbed down the aft ladder, making a short leap into the dinghy. Freeing the line that attached it to the *Innovative*, she shoved off and began yanking at the cord to the outboard motor. It sputtered again and again, but it still refused to catch. She was working instinctively now, trying to get the motor to turn over and catch, not letting herself stop to think about her actions. All her instincts were pushing her to get the hell away from Devlin, far and fast.

Suddenly, like a phantom, Jack Devlin himself rose up on the deck of the *Innovative*, just behind her. Angela turned and saw him, and an ear-splitting scream tore from her throat. Oh, God, he was alive, and he was coming after her again! Frantic with fear, she yanked as hard as she could on the outboard cord. At the same instant that Devlin launched himself into the air at the dinghy, the motor roared into life. Devlin's hands caught at the front of the little boat as Angela hit the throttle of the outboard motor. The dinghy moved forward, arched upward and around like a rearing stallion and headed directly for Jack Devlin.

The whirling motor of the outboard, a giant Mixmaster, caught Devlin and rolled right over him, its sharp rotor gashing him as it pushed him under the surface of the water. He screamed once, and disappeared. Angela didn't stop to look, she kept her hand on the throttle, pushing the little boat around until it was headed toward land. As it sped to shore, she held on tight to the side, to keep herself from toppling into the water. Now she allowed herself to look around for Devlin; she kept glancing back over her shoulder to see if he'd surfaced. But he didn't reappear. Had she killed him?

Thank God, she was almost safe! In a couple of minutes she'd be on shore, and on her way to the police. Then maybe she could start to put this nightmare behind her. As the dinghy cut through the water, Angela Bennett didn't see the sharp edges of the reef lurking below the surface, she didn't see the reef at all until it loomed up ahead of her, and by then it was already too late.

With a terrible tearing sound of splintering wood, the little dinghy slammed into the reef head on, sending Angela flying through the air. She hit the rocks hard and fell back into the ocean. As consciousness left her, her head came out of the water, bobbing up and then back down.

4

First Angela was aware only of sounds, muffled noises as though coming from a long way off. She recognized the sounds as voices, although she couldn't make out what they were saying. She tried to turn her head to hear better, but her head hurt her too much to move. Then she became aware of many points of light, blurry, but strong enough to make her wince with the pain. Angela shut her eyes again.

But gradually she realized that she was lying in a real bed, on clean sheets. Angela forced her eyes to open again, narrowing them until they became used to the overhead light. Slowly, gingerly, she turned her head and looked around. It was daytime. She appeared to be in a hospital ward, shabby with peeling paint, but antiseptically clean. She wasn't alone; she could see other patients in others beds on both sides of the room, women with the same strong, dark faces she had seen carved on Mayan pyramids. On the wall above every bed a crucifix was hanging. She must be back in Yucatan, Angela guessed, in a Catholic hospital. How did she get here? How long had she been unconscious?

Angela put her hands up to her face, which was

aching badly, and winced. She felt bumps, scratches and bruises, and one long, jagged cut over her left eye; she could make out scabs with her fingertips. Healing scabs; she must have injured herself several days ago, then. She tried to speak, but her voice came out only in a rough whisper.

'Hello?'

Nobody answered, but a nun who was tending to one of the other patients heard her and came over swiftly, skirts rustling.

'Where am I?' whispered Angela with an effort. 'How did I get here?'

'*No hablo ingles,*' the nun said sympathetically.

Angela shook her head painfully, trying to remember. Yes, it was coming back, slowly, a piece at a time. The most vivid recollection she had was her body arcing through the air in a bullet's trajectory when she hit the jagged rocks of that reef. After that, nothing more.

A Mexican doctor dressed in green scrubs came over to Angela's bed. 'Good morning. How are you feeling?'

'I . . . I'm not sure,' mumbled Angela. 'How did I get here?'

'Fishermen found you, brought you here. You were very lucky they came by,' the doctor told her in excellent Spanish-accented English.

'How . . . long . . . have I . . . been . . . ?'

'Three days.' The doctor raised one cautionary forefinger. 'Try not to talk too much. Oh, we found a man's identification on you, we tried to contact him – '

He held up Jack Devlin's wallet, which had been in Devlin's linen jacket. Right, she'd been wearing that jacket when her dinghy slammed into the rocks. Then his words registered. They'd been trying to reach Devlin! What if they had? Did he know where she was now?'

'Oh, my God, no!' cried Angela, horrified, starting up from her pillow.

'No,' the doctor shook his head sadly. 'No luck finding this man.'

Angela sank back on to the bed, weak with relief. So he was dead, then. And she was safe. A sudden thought came over her, the memory of shoving Dale's disk into the pocket next to Devlin's wallet. 'There was a disk . . . a computer disk . . . did you find it?'

'Ah, yes, there.' The doctor pointed to the small table beside Angela's bed. She propped herself up on her elbow and took a look. It was the green Mozart's Ghost disk all right, or at least, what was left of it after being exposed to salt water and the broiling hot sun. It was warped and melted, totally useless. Angela saw it with mixed feelings. As it had been so dangerous to her, she was happy to see it destroyed. It made her feel safer. But, as it represented an unsolvable mystery, she felt a pang of something akin to disappointment. She'd never solve it now.

Solve it? Was she nuts? She was no Sherlock Holmes; what Angela wanted was to get back home to the States, to Venice, to change the locks on her doors, and forget she ever knew Jack Devlin or saw this damn disk!

'It is very hot in the sun,' remarked the doctor, looking apologetically at the disk. 'Uh ... sorry, we do not know your name ... you had no identification ...'

'Angela Bennett. I'm staying at the Krystal resort. All my IDs were stolen.'

'Angela Bennett,' smiled the doctor, 'you relax now and get well. A few days and you will be –'

A few days! Angela felt a stab of real panic. 'No, No! I have to get out of here, now!' She had to get home, away from Yucatan. The urgency to leave was so strong that it drove her to throw the sheets off and get out of bed, staggering a little with a sudden fit of dizziness. 'Where are my clothes?' she pleaded. 'I need my clothes. How much do I owe you?' She grabbed up Devlin's wallet and began to pull some Mexican currency out of it.

Along with the money a small card fell out, floating on to the bed. Angela picked it up. There was no name on the card, but on it was a carefully typed out address, a strange collection of letters reading 'rcds.bnh&navDC.mil.' Angela recognized it as some kind of Internet address. There was no other kind of indentification. On the other side was printed another number, 'BER5348833'. Still a little dazed, she stuffed the card back into Devlin's wallet.

Once she was back in the lobby of the Krystal, nothing went smoothly. Angela found herself having trouble with the desk clerk, who politely but very

very firmly told her that Angela Bennett had already checked out.

'No, no, no! *I'm* Angela Bennett. I'm standing right here!' she insisted.

But the desk clerk was just as insistent. He kept shaking his head while he pointed to the computer screen. Everybody knows that computers don't tell lies. 'Angela Bennett checked out last Saturday night. She paid with a credit card. It says so right on the computer here.'

'I *didn't* check out!' If only she could get through to him! 'I would never have checked out. I didn't –' How did someone get hold of her credit card, someone who knew enough about her to check her out of her hotel? Could it be Devlin? Was he still alive?

At the rear of the lobby, a large-screen television set was playing, on the CNN News channel. Had Angela been paying attention to it, she might have learned that while she was in Mexico things had not been quiet in the States or abroad.

'International trade talks between the four nations were stalled today due to a mixup in the communications wires,' the anchor was saying. 'And now, turning to the national news . . .'

The trusted face of veteran newsman Daniel Schorr filled the screen. 'Wall Street panicked when stock prices appeared to tumble at a rate reminiscent of the Black Tuesday crash,' Schorr said gravely. 'Officials suspended trading when it became clear that the losses were fictitious and caused by computer pranksters, as obscene messages appeared on the Dow

Jones ticker. Wall Street expects to open tomorrow with its computers protected by Gregg Micro Systems' latest security program, aptly named the Gatekeeper.'

Now there was a videotape of Jeff Gregg, CEO of Gregg Micro Systems, a fair-haired young billionaire who was pushing his way through a crowd of reporters with microphones who kept shouting questions at him.

'Pranks?!' Gregg snorted. His handsome face held an expression of contempt. 'Short-sheeting someone's bed is a prank. These "cyberterrorists", as they call themselves, could have done serious damage to our economy, just as the actions at Los Angeles Airport recently could have caused a disastrous mid-air collision. Remember, information is sacred. And information is power. Society must protect that at all cost from these terrorists.'

But Angela wasn't paying attention to the TV screen, only to the computer screen at the checkin desk. It informed her definitively that Angela Bennett had checked out on Saturday. There was no arguing with the computer.

'Great!' she sighed, resigned. 'My luggage. Where's my luggage?'

'Luggage?' The desk clerk looked surprised. 'You took it with you.'

There was nothing she could say to convince him, so Angela, helpless and frustrated, turned away from the desk. Wonderful, just wonderful. She had no passport, no credit cards or any other ID, and now she didn't even have a change of clothing. All she had to wear was this blouse and skirt she'd been wearing for days, in salt water and blazing sun. At some time during her hospital stay the formerly white linen jacket belonging to a man who'd tried to kill her had disappeared. Perhaps it was too tattered to be usable, and had simply been thrown away by some hospital worker. The money in Devlin's wallet was enough to procure her a flight home, but there wouldn't be a lot left over. Still, once she was back in the States, everything would get back to normal. She'd replace her credit cards and her driver's licence and forget she'd ever been to Mexico or that a strange man named Jack Devlin had tried to kill her. But how was she to re-enter the United States without her passport?

Think, Angela, think. Okay, the United States consulate office could issue her a temporary visa. She'd call the States, Cathedral Software, and have them wire her some more money. Once she was home safe in Venice, she'd pay them back. Suddenly she wanted nothing in this world more than to see her house and her little garden with its bright bed of geraniums, to have the door shut and locked behind her, to be sitting in her own comfortable chair listening to her favourite music, putting all of this nightmare behind her.

But as she tried to place a phone call from the pay phone in the consulate lobby, using her telephone credit card number, the computerized operator gave her a hard time.

'Please dial your card number again,' announced

the transistorized voice. 'The card number you have just dialled is not valid.'

Not valid? Of course it was valid! Angela knew the number as well as she knew her own name, it was fixed in her memory, and she'd had the same number for over five years! Nevertheless, if it made the computer happy ... Grimly she punched the number in again. Once more she heard that cursed metallic voice. 'Please dial you card number –'

'Ruth Marx?' a woman's voice said behind her. 'Are you Ruth Marx?'

'No,' muttered Angela, still hassling with the phone.

'Are you the woman who's here about a temporary visa?' the voice persisted.

At those words Angela turned, seeing a consulate worker, a middle-aged woman in a tailored suit, carrying a clipboard. 'Yes, I am here about a visa, but –'

'Is your Social Security number 915-30-1717? Do you live at 39 Admirals Way, Venice, California?'

'Yeah, but –' Startled, Angela hung up the phone and looked at the clipboard. There was a photograph of her own face on the application. It was a blowup of her California driver's licence. But the name on the application was not Angela Bennett, it was Ruth Marx.

'Then, according to the computers at the California Department of Motor Vehicles, you're Ruth Marx. So, if you'll just sign your name here, we'll issue your visa.'

'But I'm not —' Angela began, and then she stopped. She needed the visa desperately; she couldn't get home without it. And the consulate was saying that it would issue it to a Ruth Marx, since that's the name they had in their files. How did a screwup like this happen? It was obviously just a computer error, one she could sort out later, when she was safely back home. Right now Angela's head still hurt badly, and she was having trouble thinking.

'You're not what?' demanded the worker impatiently.

'I'm not . . . clear about something. Without this, I can't get back into the United States. Is that correct?'

'That's correct.'

'So all I have to do is just sign Ruth Marx . . .'

'Right there.'

Angela Bennett took the pen and the application, and wrote down the unfamiliar name. Ruth Marx.

Angela remembered where she had parked her car. H4. But when she got off the shuttle bus at the LAX long-term lot, there was an RV parked in her space, its bumper plastered with pro-environmental stickers. Her own car was nowhere to be seen. Had it been towed away?

Damn it, Angela, think. Think, she told herself over and over through the throbbing in her head. What was going on here? There had to be some simple, rational explanation. But she felt that things were getting more and more strange by the minute. It was like some kind of pattern was forming. First Devlin tried to take her out, then the Ruth Marx thing, and now her car was missing. What would disappear next? Her house?

When the taxicab drew up to Angela's house on Admirals Way in Venice, dusk was already beginning to fall. It would soon be dark. But there was still enough daylight left for her to see that there was a big 'For Sale' sign on the house, reading 'Stan Whiteman, Real Estate', and the motto 'Buy the Most by the Coast'. Another sign read 'Open House'. Angela blinked in astonishment: what the hell was going on here? She felt as though she'd been hit a sharp blow in the pit of the stomach. When she'd made that grim joke to herself about her house disappearing, she had no idea that it could become a reality.

The front door was unlocked because of the open house held that day by the real estate broker. Angela opened the door slowly and stepped inside. She looked around, aghast, her eyes going wide in disbelief. The house was totally empty. Not a chair, not a pot or pan or dish, only faded carpet, some dust, a few patches on the wall where Angela's paintings had hung. Everything she owned in the world, her personal possessions, family heirlooms, her precious computers – gone. She was left with nothing, nothing.

Devastated, Angela put her hand up to her mouth to hide the trembling of her lips. 'My God,' she moaned softly to herself. Who was doing this to her? Why?

In the bathroom at the side of the house a toilet suddenly flushed, and at the sound Angela jumped nervously. She turned to go, racing toward the front door.

'Hey, don't run! Where ya runnin'? Take your time. Come in, relax.' A big, jovial man with an expensive haircut came out of the downstairs john, pulling on his jacket. 'My name's Stan Whiteman, Whiteman Realty. Come in, let me show you around. You'll like it.'

'*Like* it?' gasped Angela. '*Like* it?!' I own it! This is *my* house! What the hell are you doing here?'

The broker looked sharply at Angela. He saw a dishevelled young woman with stringy hair and shabby clothing, and a look of bewildered anger on her face. And he did what any sane realtor would do in the circumstances. He whipped out his cellular phone and called the police.

When the black-and-white pulled up, its lights flashing, Mrs Raines, the nosy next door neighbour, arrived to put her two cents in. Soon, everybody was talking at once, Angela, Stan Whiteman, the two police officers – Michael Mahoney and Herbert Kiehl – and Mrs Raines. The police were by-the-book polite, trying to referee the dispute between Angela and the real estate agent, each of whom was insisting on the legal ownership of 39 Admirals Way.

'Oh, I definitely saw her move out,' Mrs Raines eagerly contributed.

Angela whirled on her. 'You saw me? When was this?'

'Three days ago. There was a moving truck, moving men, furniture . . .'

'I've been in Mexico for the past week!' Angela yelled. 'How could I be here in Venice selling my house at the same time?' But the thought of a moving van deliberately taking away her possessions was even more upsetting to Angela. For the first time, she fully grasped the idea that there might be a conspiracy behind what was happening to her, that these were not just random errors and inconveniences. A moving-van that was real, tangible. Somebody had to have thought it up and arranged for it, somebody had to have paid for it. But who? Had Jack Devlin set it up before Cozumel, thinking he would be coming back alive and she wouldn't?

'Because it wasn't your house to sell!' Whiteman yelled back. He turned to the officers. 'It wasn't her. It belonged to a lovely woman named Angela Bennett.'

'*I'm* Angela Bennett!'

'Come on!' the real estate agent said harshly. 'The *real* Angela Bennett held the deed and the mortgage papers. Look,' he explained to the police, 'I got twenty thousand dollars sunk into my computer. We check all our records thoroughly or we don't take on a client. I checked out every record. It's not her!'

Somebody had my deed and my mortgage papers, thought Angela and her flesh crawled in horror. Somebody was out to get her, and it wasn't random, it was personal!

'Sir, please!' Officer Kiehl held up a mollifying hand. He turned to Angela. 'Ma'am, it would help everything if you could just produce *some* kind of identification.'

'You know what? I agree with you. I agree with you,' answered Angela, desperate. 'But as I have told you one thousand times already today, I had everything stolen in Cozumel.'

'Oh, please!' scoffed Whiteman. 'Ask her how she got across the border without a passport.'

'I had a temporary issued,' Angela muttered reluctantly.

'Do they do that?' shrilled Mrs Raines. 'I don't think they do that.'

'Oh, God!' She pulled out the visa, aware that the name Angela Bennett didn't appear on it anywhere. 'This is ridiculous. Here, here it is! This is it! It's just that. . . . it's under a different name.' She knew how lame that must sound, how lame anything she'd have to say from now on would sound to these people.

The officers took the visa and examined it, especially the photograph, which was definitely that of the girl in front of the. 'Is this your signature?' demanded Kiehl, pointing to the name Ruth Marx.

Angela looked increasingly uncomfortable. 'Well, it's my handwriting,' she admitted. 'But they made me sign that name.'

'Why's that?' Mrs Raines wanted to know.

Angela's brows drew together. 'Because they think I'm not me.'

'You know, it's a federal offence to forge a visa,' the neighbour said self-righteously.

'Oh, yes?' Angela's brows drew together in anger. 'And what is it to steal an entire house?'

The officer handed the visa over to his partner. 'Mike, you want to run this?'

Angela shook her head despairingly. 'It won't mean anything. They've screwed up all my records, my fingerprints . . .'

'Who's "they"?' asked Mrs Raines.

The question of the century. 'I have no idea,' Angela confessed.

'What do you do? Do you work around here?'

'Well, my office is in San Francisco, but I work out of my home.' Angela looked around in despair. Home, what home? Whoever those people were who had robbed her of her home and her car, her computers, her clothing and her identity, they sure knew what they were doing. They'd taken it all. And Angela Bennett knew for certain that somehow all of this was tied in with that Mozart's Ghost disk that Dale Hessman had sent her. That had to be the connection, what else was there? Why else would Jack Devlin have removed it from her stolen purse and thrown it into the drawer? Why else had he kept the disk and not any of her legal identification? But once he had the disk, why did he have to try to kill her? Why couldn't he just let her go?

'You don't know one person in a town the size of Los Angeles who can vouch for the fact that you're Angela Bennett?' the police officer demanded. 'A mother? A father?'

'My mother isn't well, and my father . . . no.' Angela thought a minute. For the last few years, she had been living as a virtual recluse. All her friends were out there in cyberspace. Except for one.

'There's my therapist, Alan Champion.'

'Your therapist?' the nosy neighbour asked suspiciously. The police officer raised one eyebrow. A therapist? That explained a lot.

It sounds bad I know. 'My ex-therapist.' *And that sounds worse*, thought Angela in despair.

Officer Mike Mahoney slipped behind the wheel in the black-and-white, and began to run Ruth Marx's driver's licence through his small computer hooked up to the main LAPD data banks, checking to see if there were any outstanding warrants or a police record for the strange young woman who was kicking up such a fuss inside the house. In the darkness of early evening, he didn't notice that, in a sleek black car parked across the street, a man was sitting, watching the house. And he had no idea that this man had a small computer of his own, small but state-of-the-art powerful, hooked up to a modem and linked to a vast mainframe elsewhere.

This Ruth Marx, whoever she was, was clean. She had no prior arrests, no outstanding warrants. But before officer Mahoney could call that benign information up on his police computer, the man in the car, typing busily, had broken into the police system and was changing her record radically. Now, with a few significant taps of the keys, Jack Devlin had given Ruth Marx a complete and lurid arrest record with the LAPD – petty larceny, prostitution, narcotics, parole violation. The DMV photograph scrolling across the computer screen was that of Angela Bennett. The face was the same pretty one that smiled from the Polaroid snapshot paper-clipped to the sun visor above his windshield. Devlin's souvenir.

Officer Mahoney sat scanning the small screen, reading the rap sheet, which scrolled down as long as his arm. This Ruth Marx was some piece of work. And she was wanted by the LAPD. He unhooked his two-way radio and called the precinct.

'Yeah, we got a Ruth Marx tryin' to run a scam in a house. She's wanted for prostitution and narcotics. We're goin' to bring her in.'

Through the open door Angela had a good view of the black-and-white. She saw officer Mahoney hanging up his radio phone and climbing out of the police car. Suddenly, from his stance and his hand hovering over his upholstered pistol, her instincts told her that something was very wrong, and that she might just be in real trouble here.

'Uh, can you excuse me?' Angela requested, pointing innocently in the direction of the bathroom. 'I've just got to . . . uh . . .' And she vanished.

'Mrs Raines, is she Angela Bennett or isn't she?' demanded Officer Kiehl.

'I . . . don't know . . .' Mrs Raines confessed, thoroughly confused. 'She kept to herself . . . I hardly saw her . . .'

Mike Mahoney came into the house, his holster unsnapped. 'Where's the girl?' he asked roughly.

'Where's my phone?' wailed Stan Whiteman suddenly. 'Somebody stole my phone!'

Jack Devlin, slouching in the driver's seat, sat up straight as he saw Angela Bennett running at top speed out of the side door of the house and down the darkened street. Instantly, he switched on the ignition, and started to follow her. But before he got to the end of the block, the police officers, followed by the neighbour and the real estate broker, came dashing out of the house. One of the officers, Kiehl, ran to the squad car to call in, while Mike Mahoney ran out into the road, and flagged Devlin down.

'Excuse me, sir, have you seen a young woman running out of here?' Mahoney was holding a powerful flashlight; its beam shone straight in Devlin's eyes, temporarily blinding him.

Devlin put his hand up to ward off the glare. 'No, I haven't seen anyone,' he lied calmly.

Angela ran breathlessly down the alleys that ran next to the canals. Only a few occasional street lights illuminated her flight. She had no idea of where she was going or where she could hide. She assumed the police were after her – what for she didn't know – but she had no idea that she was also being pursued by a man she thought of as dead, a man who was determined to take her life as he'd taken her identity.

Jack Devlin drove slowly, all the while glancing from one side of the road to the other, trying to catch a glimpse of a small running figure. He saw nothing, but she couldn't have gotten far. He was confident that in a few more minutes he would have her in his sights. The phone in Devlin's car rang. He picked it up at once. 'Yeah,' was all he said.

'Where's our girl going now?' asked a male voice.

'Don't worry, we'll get hold of the disk. And we'll find whoever she's been speaking to,' Devlin answered confidently. 'Don't forget, she's out there on her own, and she's feeling pretty vulnerable.'

'We don't want another Cozumel, Mr Devlin,' the voice said coldly. 'She's your responsibility. Deal with it.'

'I said I'd take care of her,' Devlin barked, and broke the connection.

A stitch in her side made Angela stop running. She looked behind her, expecting at any moment to see the lights of the police car. But she saw nothing. For the moment she seemed to be safe. Gasping for breath, she pulled out Stan Whitemore's cellphone and punched in a number.

'Cathedral Software,' the switchboard responded.

'Russ Melbourne, please.'

'Mr Melbourne is no longer with the company.'

What? What was happening? Could 'they' have gotten to him, too, as they had Dale? Angela shivered, feeling suddenly as though she was freezing. If Russ wasn't there, she had nobody to talk to. 'What do you mean? It can't be . . .'

'May I connect you to somebody who might help you?' the voice continued politely.

'I . . . I . . . never dealt with anybody else,' she stammered. 'I don't know anybody else.'

'Who may I connect you with?' the voice persisted.

She thought fast. 'The head of security systems . . . just tell them it's Angela Bennett.'

'Thank you. I'll put you through to Ms Bennett.'

'What? No . . . *I'm* Angela B – '

But she heard a ring, then a click, and a woman's voice, saying into the phone, 'Hello, this is Angela Bennett.'

Angela felt herself going into shock; she literally could not speak. She stood there on a street corner in Venice with a stolen cellphone pressed to her ear, listening to the weirdest and most terrifying thing that had happened to her since all this terrifying weirdness had begun. Someone had stolen her name; someone had stolen her *self*! Someone was pretending to be her. Who? For what purpose?

'Who is this?' she managed to gasp out at last.

'This is Angela Bennett,' the woman's voice said again. Then there was a long pause, and the woman spoke again, softly. 'This is someone who can help you. Give us the disk, Angela.'

'I don't understand. You have the wrong person. I don't know what you are talking about.'

'We're not offering you an option here,' the woman's voice went on relentlessly. 'Give us the disk, Angela, and we'll give you your life back.'

'I don't have your disk. I don't know what you mean.'

'Give us the disk, Angela,' the voice said again, and this time it held a hard edge.

But Angela heard something else as well. A series of clicks in her ear that told her that this phone call was being monitored. How and by whom she didn't know, but somebody was listening in. Instantly, she snapped the cellphone shut and took off again, at high speed.

Jack Devlin hung up the car phone; he'd had himself patched into Cathedral Software's switchboard. Good, now they knew that Angela had reached a telephone somewhere, had used it, and would be using it again. With the technology he had at his fingertips, he could easily trace her location the next time she dialled a number.

He punched in a telephone number, and spoke briefly. 'What's her number? 280-7605? Did you get the address? Good.'

5

Angela Bennett did use the phone to make another call. She was in shock at what she'd learned in her phone call to Cathedral Software, terrified, outraged and appalled at the thought that another human being was up there masquerading as herself. She had never visited her employer; no matter how many times she'd been asked up to San Francisco she'd refused, staying holed up in Venice. As a result, nobody up at Cathedral knew what she looked like or could have identified her. Now another woman was using her name and all the Cathedral Software people were accepting her as the real Angela Bennett. Now Angela had fresh evidence that 'they' were indeed after her; they had even admitted to deleting all evidence of her former life. 'Give us the disk and we'll give you your life back,' 'Angela Bennett' had told her. It wasn't a promise; Angela recognized it for what it was, a deadly threat.

Angela was shaking with anger and crying so hard that she could scarcely see the numbers on the dial. It was the knowledge that a group had been spying on her electronically, keeping her under clandestine surveillance, stripping all the details of her life away from her, which made her feel helpless and vulnerable to everything and everybody. 'They' were everywhere.

But Angela knew she couldn't afford to feel helpless, or to break down now. If ever she needed all her resources she needed them now. She had to keep her head clear, and above all, to stay a jump ahead of whoever was tracking her. With an enormous effort she pulled herself together, and dialled the telephone number of the only person in the world she could trust. Silently she begged God not to let her get his answering machine, but that's exactly what she got — his answering machine.

'Hi,' chirped the familiar voice on the tape. 'This is Dr Alan Champion. I can't get to the hone right now . . .'

'Alan! Alan!' Angela cried, her heart racing. 'Are you screening calls? Please be screening . . .' she pleaded, like a prayer.

And then, a miracle, a live voice. Alan's voice. 'Hello, hello . . . I'm here.'

'Alan, it's — ' she caught herself, remembering that her cell calls were almost certainly being monitored over some vast computer network, that she herself was being tracked. She'd better not use her name. Angela lowered her voice. 'I need your help. I'm in a lot of trouble . . .'

Jack Devlin pulled up in front of Stan Whiteman Realty. Not a live body to be seen. Not a light on anywhere inside. The brokerage office was definitely closed for the night. What the hell was going on? His contact had informed him absolutely that this was the address for the telephone Angela Bennett was using. Savagely, he punched in the phone number of his contact, and got out of the car, stretching his legs impatiently, pacing the sidewalk as he barked into his car phone. 'Are you sure this is the number we traced? Did you check the extensions? Base transfer? Call forward? Wait ... hold it a minute. Hold it.' Devlin's brain began to race. Then he had the answer; it was obvious.

Of course. I should have realized it sooner. It's not Angela's own phone. Or anybody's else's, not in a permanent location. It had to be a mobile, a cellular phone. She must have swiped it from that real estate guy whose signs were all over the yard. Devlin shook his head in admiration. 'Listen, listen. She's not using a wall phone, she's got a cellphone. Okay, no problem. Get the number ... no, don't dial it ... just put out a signal, find me two repeater cells that can pick it up, and give me the bisect. It'll find her within a few hundred yards. Go!'

Angela huddled down into the bushes at the base of the steps outside the back entrance of the church not far from Venice beach. There was a sudden burst of light above her as the door opened and the bingo players, almost all of them ladies in their fifties and sixties, flurried like chirping birds out of the church, discussing the games. Angela scrunched down a little further, so as not to be seen by them.

Headlights blinded her suddenly as a powerful car

slowly turned the corner into the church alley and came to a stop. Angela froze, one hand up to shield her eyes, peering anxiously at the car. She got ready to run.

'Angie?' a voice called.

She knew that voice. Thank God! 'Alan?'

The window of the BMW lowered, and Alan Champion's familiar bearded face leaned out, looking both puzzled and concerned. 'Angela? I hardly recognized you –'

Angela practically hurled herself into the front seat. 'Go! Go!' she urged, near hysteria. 'Just please go, Alan.'

Champion smiled, but his eyes were puzzled. 'Nice to see you, too. Hey, I'm not a cab! Say "hi".'

He was right; she was behaving like an idiot. Angela's shoulders sagged, and she returned Alan Champion's smile, although weakly. 'Hi. Thank you. Can we go now?'

Alan's smile broadened into a grin, and he reached for the gear shift. 'Yeah, now we can go.'

For a few minutes they drove in silence, following no special direction. Then Angela asked Alan, 'Do you still have that laptop I got you?'

'I'm wearing it,' he joked.

'I'm serious. We've got to get it. Then, could you take me to a hotel room?'

He glanced at her sideways. 'Now that's do-able,' he said mildly, with one raised eyebrow and a mock leer.

Angela shook her head. Still immature old Alan. He

hadn't changed. There was something reassuring about that. And something just a little exasperating. 'Alan, let's just go. . . .'

Jack Devlin homed in tightly on the cellphone, using the coordinates his confederates had established for him. The signal was very strong; the phone was now in use and it wasn't far away. Within the next minute or two he would have Angela Bennett right where he wanted her, staring down the business end of a 9mm pistol.

His car drew close to the curb as the bisecting signals triangulated, giving him the phone's location. Yes, there it was! But where was his Angela? Instead, Devlin saw a homeless man, pushing all of his meagre belongings ahead of him in a grocery cart chatting on the cellphone as he walked along. Angela had junked it, simply throwing it away where she knew someone else would find and use it. She'd done it to put him off the scent.

'Clever girl,' Devlin murmured to himself, amused by her ingenuity. But his eyes narrowed, glittering coldly. He was not pleased.

They stopped off at Alan Champion's apartment only long enough to retrieve the laptop and pack a few pieces of clothing his ex-wife hadn't bothered to take when they split up. Angela desperately needed to change out of her grungy shirt and skirt. But she wouldn't do it there. 'They' might already have connected her to Alan. 'They' had their methods. No, she insisted on the anonymity of a hotel, and right away.

To humour her Dr Alan Champion went along with whatever she wanted; it was obvious to him that Angela was very close to breaking point. She had always been timid with people, afraid of life, and as both her shrink and her lover, he had seen her before at her most vulnerable. But he had never seen her in a state like this, nervous to the point of paranoia, jumping out of her skin at every sudden sound or movement. She didn't even look like herself. The Angela Bennett he remembered was soft and needy, a fatherless fawn, a homeless kitten. This woman was strung as tightly as a concert violin; there was no softness about her at all. Her face was drawn, almost hollow, her cheekbones standing out like sharp knives. There were smudged shadows under her eyes, and the eyes themselves appeared haunted, as though they'd been looking at horrors.

Dr Alan Champion had seen many delusional and paranoid patients in his psychiatric practice. He was all too familiar with the concept of 'they', that unidentified menacing group out to get the innocent. 'They' were always omnipotent and all-knowing, evil gods whose deadly purpose it was to track down their victim and destroy him. 'They' had invisible methods and powerful means by which they could spy on their victim without being detected. And 'they' were always bound together in a conspiracy against the victim. There are always more men and women than you think walking around in hats lined with aluminium foil so that spy satellites or microwaves or alien intelligences can't get at their brains. Alan Champion had never expected that Angela Bennett would ever be one of them.

But these were the very thoughts – conspiracy, surveillance, altering of life records – that she was expressing to him. She was talking about 'they' and 'them' as though they were totally real. It was painful for him to watch Angela, whom in his own way he had never stopped loving, falling prey to paranoid fantasies such as the ones she was running away from. Whatever she believed, it had taken its toll on her. She was dazed, whitefaced, exhausted, and almost inarticulate. Alan's heart ached to see her this way.

As soon as they came into the hotel room he rented – for cash, not a credit card, as Angela had insisted – she ran to the windows and pulled the drapes tightly shut, even though the large living room looked out on the beach and the ocean.

Angela turned from the window. 'You don't have to stay if you don't want to. I'm sure that what's her name – '

'Amy,' supplied Alan. 'Don't worry. That's over with.'

'I'm sorry,' said Angela.

'Don't be. We're not.' Alan headed for the honour bar, opened the small fridge and poked his head inside. 'I never thought I'd hear from you again.'

'I thought you'd be safe,' she said simply.

100

Standing up, he grinned at her a little bitterly. 'Ah, so I went from being a self-centered asshole to being safe. Thank you very much.'

Angela shrugged. 'I figured they couldn't trace me to you. Your patient records are confidential, right?'

His mouth twisted in disappointment. 'My patient records,' he said flatly. So that's all she needed him for. 'I knew I had my subtle charms.'

'You're the only one I have to turn to right now.' Angela's voice cracked; her huge dark eyes welled up as she fought back the tears. And there it was, Angela's old familiar softness. Alan found himself inexpressibly moved.

'You know what? I'm going to take that as a big, big compliment.' He stood up from the bar, brandishing two small individual bottles of gin. 'Guess what time it is. Gibsons . . . almost. We don't have any onions. Well, we'll just have to use these.' Reaching into his jacket pocket, he pulled out a small prescription bottle. 'Seldane, antihistamine of champions.' He grinned at the pun.

Angela shook her head. 'I'll pass.' Nevertheless, she did laugh a little.

'I could always make you laugh,' said Alan, and he swallowed the pill with a slug of the gin. Weather like this, when the hot winds swept through Southern California and distributed pollens from trees and weeds, always played hell with Alan's allergies, Angela remembered. He would chew up antihistamines as if they were Lifesavers.

Holding the gym bag out to her, Alan Champion

said, 'I come bearing gifts. Some of Amy's clothes. I hope they fit.'

Distracted, Angela accepted the clothes, but it was plain her thoughts were elsewhere. She turned her eyes up to Alan's, and he thought he had never seen her more unhappy, more touchingly vulnerable. 'This is such a nightmare, Alan. It's like I'm not me anymore,' she whispered.

He couldn't stand it. She was weirding him out. Taking a couple of steps toward her, Alan grabbed Angela by her shoulders, and looked deeply into her eyes. 'Look at me,' he insisted as she tried to turn her face away. 'You're freaking me! If you're not you, who do you think you are?'

Furious, Angela pulled herself away. God, what did he think? That she was nuts, that she didn't have both oars in the water, that she was experiencing hallucinations? 'You're not listening, Alan!' She grabbed up the clothes and headed for the bathroom to wash up and change.

'I've heard every word,' he called after her. 'Someone stole your purse –'

She stopped in the doorway to the bathroom, and looked at him wordlessly. Then she shut the door behind her, saying only, 'I didn't expect you to believe me.'

Alan Champion was stung by the disappointment in Angela's tone. He realized that he'd let her down badly. He came up to the bathroom door and raised his voice so she could hear him. 'I believe you. I believe you're still a very scared woman, largely disconnected from the world, with being in touch with people . . . your father leaving . . .'

The bathroom door swung open and now a furious Angela was suddenly in his face, her eyes blazing. 'Don't you pull that crap on me, doctor! My father has nothing to do with why my car is missing, my father has nothing to do with why my house has been emptied, or why the entire Los Angeles police force is chasing after me –'

Shamefaced, Alan shrugged awkwardly. 'Look, I'm not saying something isn't happening to you, but all this doesn't make any sense. I don't want to be simplistic, Angie . . . but you just seem to be reaching out –'

'You know what?' Angela cried angrily. 'I am! I am reaching out, for someone who knows me, who will listen to me, who will believe me, who'll be my friend.' She turned away from him, her eyes filling up with tears. 'I thought that was you,' she added in a low tone.

Her words struck a nerve. 'Angie, I'm sorry.' Alan moved toward her and took her arm gently, turning her back around to face him. 'Sometimes it's easier for me to play doctor than it is to listen.'

She turned her tear-stained face up to his. 'I don't understand,' she cried in a near-wail. 'Why me? Why me?! I'm nobody, there's no reason . . . Alan, I'm telling you they knew! They knew everything about me, what I ate, drank, the movies I watched, where I came from, even the brand of cigarettes I used to smoke –' She broke off, as all at once the full realization hit her like a blow to the chest. 'It's the Net,' she breathed, her eyes going wide. 'They must have watched everything I did on the Net, followed my credit cards. Our whole lives are on computer! They knew they could disappear me, that they could take it all . . .'

The conviction in her voice was very disturbing to Alan Champion. Either Angela was telling the truth, or she had constructed a delusion so real that it had taken control of her life and was driving her out of her mind. But if her story was true, it presupposed a conspiracy so bizarre, so widespread and so menacingly deadly that it defied rational belief. As Angela herself said, she was a nobody. Why her? Who would want to do something so monstrous to an innocent girl like Angela Bennett? It just didn't make sense.

'It's okay,' he assured her, holding her and patting her on the back as one would a crying child. 'It's okay.' But in his heart Dr Alan Champion was not at all certain that it was okay.

'Alan, I need you to move my mother, but under another name,' Angela said suddenly, her face grim. 'Anywhere, but under another name. Get her out of Oaktree Manor before they find her. You're a doctor, no one would question it. I'm afraid of what these people might do.'

Alan looked sharply at her; to him Angela now appeared to be quite lucid and in deadly earnest. 'I guess I could move her to the County Sanitarium,' he answered slowly. 'I could say she's needed for observation.'

For the first time, Angela's face seemed to relax. 'It

would mean a lot to me,' she told him gratefully. 'She's all I've got.'

'There really is something going on here, isn't there?' he asked her seriously.

Angela nodded without a word.

'Okay,' said Alan, drawing in his breath. 'I'm not saying I buy the whole package, but ... I know this guy over at the Federal Building, Ben Phillips, with the FBI. I'll give him a call, get some answers.'

'You trust him?' asked Angela quickly.

'Absolutely,' Alan Champion grinned reassuringly. 'I used to hold his head over the toilet at frat parties. He owes me. Okay. I'm going home to formulate a plan for moving your mother. Then I'll call Ben. If I get any information, I'll get back to you.'

Suddenly, Angela didn't want him to go; she didn't want to be alone. But she knew that what she had to do next was so confidential, so vitally important, and so potentially dangerous that she couldn't possibly get Alan involved, no matter how much she trusted him. She nodded assent, smiling at him with trembling lips, and he pulled her into his arms and hugged her to him, enjoying the familiarity of her body pressed close to his. He'd missed her a lot. Crazy or sane, he was happy to see her again, happy that Angela had turned to him when she needed someone.

'Hey, it's going to be okay,' he whispered reassuringly. 'I'm on watch now.' Hugging her even more tightly, Alan couldn't help adding. 'This wouldn't have happened if you'd stayed with me.' Then, knowing he'd said a little too much, he stepped back and let her go.

As he reached the door, Angela called after him. 'Alan?' He turned. 'Thank you for everything,' she said with quiet sincerity.

He grinned at her, the jaunty old Alan-grin she knew so well. 'You're welcome. You stay put, kiddo.' And he was gone.

The promise of safety for her mother was the first thing that gave Angela the chance to relax. She took a long bath, and then, wrapped in the terry cloth robe that she found hanging in the hotel bathroom, she lay down for a short nap. But, in her exhaustion, Angela slept for many hours. She woke up rested and hungry, and determined to find out what was happening.

A few minutes later, Angela Bennett, dressed in another woman's shirt and jeans, was sitting at a laptop computer, holding an Internet address in her hands, 'rcds.bnh@navDC.mil,' the address on the card in Devlin's wallet. She knew she had a hard job ahead of her. She couldn't enter the Net by the front door. They'd be waiting for her, intercepting as soon as she accessed the Net address. She'd have to go in through the servant's entrance, using a different 'packet'.

That meant she'd have to detour down an international pathway, skipping from one country to the next to defy detection and confuse anybody watching out for her. No matter how alert 'they' were, or how guarded, these tactics would probably slow them down and gain her some time. A computer had gotten her into this mess; now she was counting on a computer to help get her out of it. This was where she felt the most confident, surfing through the Internet with her hands firmly on the keyboard. This was Angela Bennett's natural environment, where her expertise was her greatest strength.

Pieces were beginning to fall into place. Everything 'they' had done to her so far had been accomplished through the criminal alteration of computer records. They were breaking the law using the Internet as their unwitting accomplice. Angela's driving licence was in the computer; her car's licence plate was in the computer; her credit cards were in the computer; her automatic teller card that gave her the access to her checking account, the number of her safe deposit box that held her important documents like her bank mortgage and the deed to her home, these were all in a database somewhere. The computer could tell exactly what Angela Bennett was worth – how much she had in checking and savings, what her monthly car and mortgage payments were, how much equity she had in her home; what she spent her money on; what software she'd bought for her computers; even who her friends were.

In George Orwell's apocalyptic novel *1984* he wrote 'Big Brother is watching you.' But Orwell in his vision of the future did not imagine, could not imagine a future in which there were thousands of Big Brothers ... hundreds of thousands ... armed with nothing more than a keyboard and a password, and all of them watching you. Every time you make a purchase, they see. When you fill your prescription at the local pharmacy, make a bank deposit or an ATM transaction, pay your utility bills, apply for a passport, buy a seat on a plane, a thousand thousand Big Brothers are watching you.

As Orwell had predicted, privacy was now a thing of the past. Cyberspace snooping is a commonplace today. Anyone wanting to could get hold of Angela Bennett's personal data; any fifteen-year-old hacker with a sophisticated computer and the right software could gain access to almost every facet of Angela Bennett's life. But 'they' were no teenage computer hackers breaking into the high school's computers to change their grades. 'They' had apparently inexhaustible means, cutting-edge methods and a determination that was deadly. They could accomplish infinitely more than an army of hackers. But for what motive? What did they hope to gain by robbing her of her life? And, most important, who the hell were 'they'?

Angela's screen lit up with the words, 'L'Internet Suisse, Bonjour.' Welcome to the Swiss Internet.

'*Merci*,' grinned Angela. 'Now prompt me.'

And there it was, the prompt, a pulsing cursor.

'Okay, Devlin, you carried this around with you, so it must be important,' murmured Angela, and she typed in the address on the card.

The screen beeped twice, the message read, 'Connecting,' and the next thing Angela knew she was staring at the seal of the US Navy, and the logo of the Medical Records Department of Bethesda Naval Hospital.

'Bethesda Naval Hospital?' murmured Angela,

puzzled. The computer was now asking politely for her password for further access.

Angela turned the card over and looked at the number written on the back, BER5348833. 'I'll try you,' and she typed it in. Immediately, the computer refused it, declaring it invalid. Hmmmm. Angela sat back in her chair and thought for a second or two. Then she noticed the small Greek letter *pi*, in the lower right corner of the screen. This she had seen before.

'You look familiar. Let's see if you work,' she said, mouse-clicking on it, and all at once the screen went nuts, and demanded her password again, this time less politely. Once more, Angela typed in the BER number, and this time it seemed to work, because she found herself accessing a program of medical records labelled 'Highly Confidential'.

These were the medical records of the late Undersecretary of Defense Michael Bergstrom, and they declared that, based on the autopsy reports, Bergstrom had been mis-diagnosed. He was *not* HIV-positive; he showed no sign at all of HIV infection. Here was a strange piece that Angela couldn't fit into the puzzle . . . yet . . . but she recognized it as a puzzle piece, and an important one.

'Oh my God,' she breathed. For some reason, 'they' had murdered the Undersecretary of Defense of the United States just as surely as if they had held the gun that blew his head off. Just like 'they' had murdered Dale Hessman just as surely as if they had shot his plane down out of the sky. 'They' had sent Jack Devlin to find her and kill her; 'they' were still after her.

And now she knew that 'they' had to be connected in some way to the little Greek letter she'd seen on every computer program she had called up, from Mozart's Ghost to the Department of the Navy. *Pi*, that's who 'they' were, *pi*.

Now Angela knew what, she almost knew who, but she was still fuzzy about why. What did they have to gain? If she could find out, it might help her to get her life back.

The car phone in Devlin's car rang. 'Someone's on,' his contact's flat anonymous voice told him.

'Think it's our girl?' asked Devlin. He waited tensely for the answer.

'Whocvcr it is, they're covering their tracks bigtime. They've made a dozen hops so far. A POP in Switzerland, the little Unix box at the University of Montana, five different routers at Berkeley . . .'

Oh, yes. It was her, all right. His clever little Angela. A thin smile tugged the corners of Devlin's lips. He couldn't help admiring her smarts. It made the game all the more interesting, and the inevitable outcome would be all the more satisfying. Devlin glanced down at the small computer on the front seat of his car. An international routing map on the screen was mirroring the search for Angela being conducted on the mainframe.

'How long will it take to track her?' he demanded of his contact.

'Depending how much she sets up, and how long

she stays on, fifteen minutes ... half an hour at the most.'

'Call me the second you find her.'

'And that ... other matter, Mr Devlin?' the voice asked delicately.

'Free of charge.'

Alan Champion thumbed through the new magazines on the racks while he waited for his pharmacist to refill his Seldane prescription. His head was really stuffed and he was finding it hard to catch his breath. *Next year I get those allergy shots*, he swore to himself.

The pharmacist took the empty bottle and ran his laser pen over the barcode on the label. The pen was linked to his database; its reading was entered into his computer, where the data on all his customers' prescriptions was stored. Instantly, the computer brought up Dr Champion's file. The pharmacist consulted the screen. It said that Dr Alan Champion was entitled to three more refills on his prescription. The name 'Seldane' did not appear on the screen anywhere.

Five minutes later, the druggist handed the little bottle over the counter to his customer in a sealed bag. 'Here you go, Dr Champion.'

Once out on the street, Alan found it more difficult than ever to breathe. He tore the bag open, wrestled the childproof cap off the medicine bottle and swallowed down a pill. The street was dark, and he didn't read the label on the bottle. But then, there was no reason to.

Angela Bennett turned to her only friends for help, accessing her Cyber Chat bulletin board on the Net. But as she typed in her password, doubts began to flood over her. Wait a minute! Whom could she trust? In her own chat corner were Iceman, Gandalf and Cyberbob, the three Net users with whom she'd had almost nightly electronic conversations for more than a year. In cyberspace, they were her buddies, but what did she really know about them? Time to find out more.

'Who is Iceman?' she typed, clicking on his icon, a little skull.

At once, the screen scrolled the information. Angela smiled. Iceman, aka Kelly Mann, was twelve years old. No threat there, but also not much help. What about Gandalf? 'Who is Gandalf?' she typed. The data scrolled. Gandalf was thirty-seven years old, but he lived thousands of miles away in India. Again, no threat and no help. This left only Cyberbob, the most paranoid, intelligent and savvy of Angela's cyberpals. His personal icon was a little clownish face with its tongue sticking out, as though it were dead. Angela mouse-clicked on the face.

'Who is Cyberbob?' she asked her computer.

And his personal data appeared suddenly before Angela's eyes. Cyberbob, aka Robert Fox, thirty-nine years old, with an address in West Hollywood. He lived near enough to possibly be of help to her. Near enough to be part of the conspiracy? She had to take the chance. *Please let him be online*, she prayed, and typed his name and her message.

'Cyberbob, I need your expertise, please. Meet me in private room.' Private room was a space on the net chat line where electronic conversations could be held without others eavesdropping on their computers. She entered without using her icon, a little Angel, because she wanted to remain anonymous, and a few seconds later the screen showed her Cyberbob's little clown face.

Computers were Cyberbob's life. Of course he was online, where else would he be? And he seemed to be eager to help his buddy Angel.

'Have you ever seen a *pi* symbol attached to a program?' typed Angela.

There was a pause, and then this message appeared. '*Pi* = Praetorians.'

'The Praetorians?' typed Angela. 'Who are they?'

'The Big Bad Wolf,' answered Cyberbob, 'cyberterrorists, technocrooks, they want to blow the house down.'

'Cyberbob, I need more information.'

'LAX, Wall Street, Atlanta, extremely dangerous, Angel, don't mess with them.'

It's a little late for that, Angela thought ruefully. And then, *Atlanta? What happened in Atlanta?* She'd been on the run since early yesterday evening, and had not read or watched any news. 'Can't help it,' she typed in quickly. 'They're messing with me.'

'Must not continue. Must meet IRL. In private.'

IRL. 'In real life,' Angela whispered aloud. 'In private.' No, she didn't dare take the risk of a private meeting. She knew nothing about this Bob Fox. She

113

typed, 'No, somewhere safe, somewhere with a lot of people around...' She thought a few seconds, mentally picturing the nearby stretch of California beach, her mind scanning for the right meeting place. She had it.

'Where?' typed Cyberbob.

'The Santa Monica pier. By the ferris wheel.'

'Agreed,' typed Cyberbob. 'Seven o'clock tonight. I'll be wearing – '

A beeping noise on Angela's computer interrupted them, and an error message appeared suddenly on the screen. 'Communication Link Dropped.' They'd been disconnected. Damn. Well, she'd have to find Cyberbob somehow. She took a quick glance at her watch; it was close to seven now. She'd have just enough time for a quick shower. Angela was so excited speculating about what Cyberbob might have to tell her that she never stopped to wonder how come they'd been disconnected. Or by whom.

Angela was drying her hair when the telephone began to ring. Over the noise of the hotel's hair dryer she didn't hear it ringing until almost a minute had passed. As soon as she heard it, she went to pick up the receiver, but whoever it was phoning her had already hung up. Angela stood with the receiver in her hand. Who knew she was here? Only Alan. In fact it *was* Alan, calling from the lobby.

But it might well have been Jack Devlin. The Praetorians had successfully tracked Angela's laptop across the Internet miles to the hotel room where she was holed up. He knew exactly what she had planned, where she was going, and whom she was expecting to meet. His car phone rang.

'Any luck?'

'8833 Rosewood, West Hollywood.'

A dark sharklike grin spread widely across Devlin's chiselled features. 'Remind me to buy you guys something nice.'

6

The sudden loud banging on her hotel-room door made Angela's heart leap into her throat. 'C'mon, open up! Angie, you there? Open the door, I'm dying here with these bags.'

Running to the door, Angela peered through the little glass peephole. She saw Alan; he was carrying a number of heavy plastic bags, and he was alone. Hastily pulling the chain off the lock, she threw the door open. 'Alan, I'm sorry . . . I thought maybe . . .'

'Hey, take it easy! No problem. I figured you might be hungry so I stopped on the way over and I got your favourite, Chinese.'

God, he never changed! Angela shook her head, half irritated, half amused. 'It's *your* favourite. I never cared for Chinese food, remember?'

Alan smiled and shrugged. 'Well, I knew it was somebody's.'

Taking the towel and the hair dryer to the bathroom, Angela called over her shoulder. 'Is my mother okay?'

'Safely ensconced at County. She's fine, absolutely fine. Listen, Angie, I'm sorry about the Chinese, let me make it up to you. Why don't we go over to that

Greek restaurant we used to like?' By calling up the old days, Alan was very obviously trying to get one foot in Angela's emotional door. But right now, Angela wasn't home; she had other, more important fish to fry.

Angela tied her sneakers, and began pulling on a short denim jacket. She shook her head no. 'I can't. I've got to go,' she said hurriedly.

'Really? Why do you have to go?' he complained. 'Every time I see you now you're running away.' Alan sounded aggrieved, and more than a little hurt.

Angela shook her head. 'No, I'm not running away. It's just a guy I'm meeting, a friend from the Internet. He knows what's going on – '

'Hold on!' interrupted Alan, scowling. 'Let's take it easy here. Don't always be in such a rush. So listen, can I at least tell you about my friend Ben Phillips, the FBI guy you wanted to talk to? I called him; he was very interested. Ben wants to see you first thing in the morning. Did you hear me? Angie, can't you wait?'

But Angela was already heading for the door. 'And did your friend know about LAX and Wall Street and whatever happened in Atlanta?' she demanded.

'What, the blackout last night?' Alan laughed scornfully. 'Some kids just shut down most of the lighting grid, spelling "Braves Suck" from the air. Is that supposed to be a national emergency?'

But Angela hardly heard him. 'Alan, Cyberbob knows what's going on,' she told him seriously. 'He's figured it out. If we wait, it might be too late – '

'Just *listen* to you!' cried Alan Champion, frustrated. 'You're meeting someone named *Cyberbob*? Have you ever met this guy?'

She knew what he was trying to tell her. A name like Cyberbob did sound foolish if you didn't know the people of the Internet. Unable to answer, Angela looked away, and Alan suddenly realized that she was genuinely terrified and that he wasn't making things better. 'Okay, okay,' he soothed her. 'These are your friends, I know that. But I don't want you going alone.'

'Why don't you come with me, then?'

'Sure I will.' At once, Alan was rewarded by Angela's sudden bright smile, grateful for his help. Her face was still as lovely when she smiled as it had always been. Alan felt suddenly warm.

'Where are we meeting him?'

'Santa Monica pier.'

Driving south along the ocean road toward the Santa Monica pier, Alan began to feel warmer, uncomfortably warmer. He loosened his necktie as Angela tried to explain to him the incredible scope of the conspiracy, a scope she hadn't quite yet grasped herself.

'These people are dangerous,' Angela insisted. 'They killed Dale because of what he found. Now they think I have this program – '

'Angie, look, I'm with you on this, but first you say someone tried to kill *you*, and now this guy Dale – '

'They've also put someone in my place at Cathedral to get rid of any traces there,' Angela continued.

Alan shook his head to clear it of fuzziness. It was feeling heavy, almost swollen. 'I'm missing something here,' he said slowly.

'They'd want someone in Cathedral's mainframe, to set traps, overwrite programs, to make sure it won't happen again, that nobody else will be able to break into their system and see what they're doing. It could take weeks, you can't do that from outside.'

But Alan could hardly hear her; he was trying to hold on to the BMW's steering; the car was threatening to veer from the roadway on to the sidewalk because he wasn't quite seeing straight. He was sucking in air, and with each attempt it became more and more difficult to catch his breath. Why wasn't the Seldane working? Surely it ought to have kicked in by now. This was some mother of an allergy attack! 'Why . . . why would they be doing all this?'

'I've got no idea,' confessed Angela. 'But the Internet number I told you this guy Devlin had? I plug it in and suddenly I'm staring at the private medical records of Undersecretary of Defense Michael Bergstrom.'

'Bergstrom? The guy . . . who . . . blew . . . his head off?' Alan asked with an effort. His tongue felt strangely thick.

'A computer blood test told him he had AIDS. But when they did the autopsy, there wasn't a trace of HIV.' Angela laughed bitterly, a short, sharp bark of a laugh. 'Well, who knows? Maybe when they do my autopsy I can finally prove I'm not really Ruth Marx.'

Alan looked over at Angela. 'You know what's

frightening me? I'm beginning to ... think ... that maybe you're not delusional.' A wave of nausea swept over him suddenly. His heart began to pump faster. What could have caused this? Suddenly, he knew. This was no allergy attack, he realized in panic. This had all the earmarks of a fullblown anaphylactic reaction. He was going into anaphylactic shock. And anaphylaxis is often fatal. With trembling fingers he groped for the pill bottle on the dashboard. He squinted to read the label. Oh, Jesus! No!

Angela was thinking fast now. 'You know what I've got to do, Alan? I've got to go to San Francisco, get up to Cathedral, get on that Mozart's Ghost's program, 'cause that's gotta be it. That has to be it. They've got that echo system on every computer. They use it to trace your keystrokes in case you've made a mistake – '

Angela broke off as Alan began to cough heavily. She looked across the seat at him. He was racked with coughs and beads of sweat were running down his face.

'Alan! Are you all right? What's the matter?' He seemed to be losing control of the car, which was dangerously close to the yellow line down the middle of the road. Before Angela could get to the wheel, the BMW began to swerve, jumped the line, bumped up on the curb, crashed into a garbage can, and came to rest on the sidewalk.

'Alan! Alan! What is it?' Angela leaned over to peer at him; he looked terrible. His breath was coming in painful rasping gasps, and he was painfully trying to talk, to tell her something.

120

'The . . . pills . . .'

'Alan, what is it? What pills? Oh, God, Alan!' He couldn't answer, couldn't speak. He was pale, he was choking, his entire body was shaking. To Angela, it looked very much like Alan Champion might be dying.

Cyberbob and the meeting at the Santa Monica pier were now totally forgotten. The only thing on Angela Bennett's mind was that she had to get Alan Champion to the emergency room before he died. She pushed Alan over to the passenger seat and climbed behind the wheel. Her heart pounded with fear as she drove. She went through red lights without noticing them, turned the wrong way down one-way streets, drove at eighty in a thirty-mile-an-hour residential zone.

Beside her, Alan was losing consciousness. He was very pale and weak, and his breath came in shallow gasps.

'I'll get you to the hospital,' Angela promised.

'The . . . pills,' he mumbled again. And then he passed out, slumping in his seat.

Oh, God! Oh, God! We've got to get there in time! At last she pulled the BMW up to the ambulance entrance of the hospital. 'Help me!' she yelled. 'Help me, please!'

Two attendants came running out with a stretcher, and they wheeled Alan away. They wouldn't let her follow him into the examination room. For twenty minutes she sat suffering outside the nurses' station, waiting for news of Alan. At last she approached the desk.

'He's going to be all right, isn't he?' she asked the nurse.

The RN typed a few keys and Alan Champion's file came up on her computer. 'He's allergic to penicillin,' she informed Angela. 'They've got him intubated and pumped full of epinephrine.'

Angela looked at her helplessly. 'I have no idea what you just said,' she confessed. But penicillin? She knew that Alan Champion couldn't tolerate that drug. Wasn't it Seldane he was taking? Then she remembered him mumbling, 'the pills . . .'

The nurse smiled. 'He'll be fine,' she assured Angela with sympathy. 'If you like, you can go see him now.'

Gratitude and relief made Angela's face light up. 'Thank you,' she breathed.

She came quietly into his room. Alan Champion was hooked up to an intravenous drip with a monitor recording his vital signs, but he was already looking a little more like his old self. His eyes were shut, but there was some colour returning to his face, and he appeared to be breathing normally again.

'Hey, how you feeling?' whispered Angela.

Alan opened his eyes, smiling weakly at the sight of her. 'I'm starving,' he whispered back.

What a relief, he was coming back to normal. Angela approached the bed and sat down close to him. 'The minute you get out, I'll cook you the best microwave meal you ever had,' she promised.

'How long are they gonna keep me here?'

'Just another day.'

Alan grinned. 'Will you be handling the out-patient care, nurse?'

Angela returned his smile. She was so relieved to see him alive that a feeling of joy, totally unexpected, suddenly raced through her. 'Do you mind?' she whispered tenderly.

'Mmmm mmm. Visions of sponge baths dance in my head.'

Angela glanced at her wristwatch. It was a few minutes past seven; she was already late. 'Look, I've got to go. Are you gonna be okay?'

'I'll be fine,' he whispered. 'I'm more worried about you.'

'I'll be fine,' she echoed. Then, 'I wish this was over.'

'I know,' Alan said softly. His eyes were beginning to drift shut, but he fought the sleepiness off. 'Hey, come closer, I want to tell you something.

Angela leaned in, and Alan gave her a clumsy kiss, half on her cheek, half on her eyebrow. 'I've been wanting to do that since yesterday,' he murmured.

The little kiss released something in Angela, an echo of the deep tenderness she used to feel for Alan; for too long it had lain buried, but now it came out again. She laid her head on his shoulder, cuddling next to him, luxuriating in the first human touch, the first closeness since this nightmare had begun. She'd almost forgotten how to feel. 'Get better,' she whispered to Alan. 'I might let you do it again.'

Alan stroked her shoulders and back lightly and sleepily, but his gentle fingertips told Angela that she was still dear to him. For a long moment they stayed like this, Angela nestling on Alan's shoulder. But if her body was at rest for now, her brain wasn't. She couldn't help thinking of what was out there waiting for her. If only this moment could go on forever. Here, with Alan, she could persuade herself that she was safe! But Angela knew her safety was an illusion; it couldn't last and wasn't really true. As much as Angela wanted to stay here with Alan, she had to get back out there; she was still on the run, and she had a vital appointment to keep.

Reluctantly, she pulled herself away from Alan's encircling arms and stood up to go. 'Do you still think I'm crazy?' she asked him softly.

He smiled sleepily and fondly at her. 'Sure. I always have.'

At the door, Angela turned to look at him one last time. Alan Champion was asleep, still with a smile on his face.

About an hour after Angela left, the night nurse made his rounds, pushing a utility cart that held medication for his floor, little paper cups holding the stipulated doses of pills and capsules, and bags of intravenous solutions for the drips. He had a chart on a clipboard, a computer printout showing all the patients' names, the necessary meds and the dosages. He stopped at the foot of Alan's bed, and scanned his printout with a laser pen, checking against the hospital ID bracelet on Alan's wrist. Then he took an IV sac off the cart and attached it to the tube in Alan's arm. Tossing the old IV into a metal pan on the lower shelf of his cart, and whistling under his breath, the nurse wheeled off to the next patient.

In his sleep, Alan Champion moaned slightly. The intravenous fluid began to drip, drip into his vein.

It was 7:27; she was almost half an hour late. Angela pushed through the crowds on the pier looking for Cyberbob. She had no idea of what he looked like, and she would be unfamiliar to him as well, but she kept moving in the direction of the ferris wheel, where they had agreed to meet. In her intense scanning of the crowds for a face that might be Cyberbob's, Angela Bennett seemed to have lost sight of the fact that she was actually pushing her way through crowds of people, one of her worst fears. In the laughing mob of pleasure seekers she felt safer than she would have on an empty stretch of beach. This was a very different Angela Bennett from the girl who'd hugged the wall at LAX less than two weeks earlier. Whatever else she might fear, she was no longer afraid of these innocent children and happy men and women who were simply out for a good time and a few laughs.

The pier was very crowded this warm evening. The thrill rides were packed with children and adults; the refreshment stands had long lines waiting for hot dogs, cold drinks, and soft ice cream. Balloon sellers were everywhere, and mylar balloons in the shape of cartoon figures and hearts bobbed colourfully over the throng. Loud music blared from all sides. A clown in a bright pink plush rabbit suit, complete with long ears and buck teeth, wandered through the crowd, teasing and tickling the delighted children, annoying the grownups.

When she reached the ferris wheel Angela peered around for somebody who might be Cyberbob, a man in his late thirties who looked as though he was waiting to meet someone. She saw no one who fitted this description. But as she searched the faces of the people, an arm suddenly wrapped around her from behind, pinning her tightly. Angela whirled, and found herself looking into the handsome, evil face of Jack Devlin. She uttered a cry of surprise and fear.

Devlin! So he wasn't dead! Somehow, somewhere deep inside herself, Angela had never believed that she was really free of him. Ever since she'd realized that she was being followed, stalked by a menace, even after she'd learned that the menace was the the Praetorians, she had associated them with Jack Devlin. In her mind 'they' had always worn the sardonic face and mocking smile of Jack Devlin.

'It's safer to stay right here,' Devlin said pleasantly. But his arm tightened around her. 'Sorry Bob couldn't make it,' he whispered into Angela's horrified ear.

Oh, God! Cyberbob! They'd got to him too. Devlin had no compunction about pulling a trigger, so the poor guy was surely dead, and it was her fault. She ought to have stayed away from him, not dragged him into this terrible business. Sick at heart, Angela tried to pull away, but Devlin was far too strong for her. Wildly, she swung her free arm through the air, hoping to land a punch, but Devlin only laughed and grasped her even more strongly.

'I hope this isn't how you greet all your old lovers,' he said lightly.

Instantly, Angela's fear turned to fury. Lovers! How dared he! Nothing could ever erase the shameful memory of her throwing herself into this man's arms; she would carry the stain of it all her life. But he had responded to her approach, making love to her with convincing passion, all the while knowing that he planned to shoot her dead. Angela slapped at him ineffectually; Devlin warded her blows off with ease. 'Not exactly the category *you* fit into,' she yelled. 'I'm surprised you didn't kill me *then* fuck me!'

Suddenly Devlin's hand grabbed the back of Angela's head by her hair, bringing her face very close to his. His voice was low and harsh. 'Listen,' he hissed through clenched teeth. 'It was difficult, right? Because I was genuinely attracted to you. I still am.'

Angela stared back defiantly. 'I'm going to genuinely attract the attention of half the Santa Monica police department at the top of my lungs if you don't let go of me *right now*!' She saw a couple of police officers standing only ten yards away, watching the throngs of people.

Jack Devlin smiled and took his arms away from Angela. He put his hands up in a sarcastic gesture of mock surrender. 'Oh, yes? You've been avoiding them ever since you ran out of the house.'

So Jack Devlin had been following her for days; that must have been *his* interference she'd detected on the cellphone. It must have been Devlin who had tracked her computer, Devlin who had disconnected her call to Cyberbob. Devlin knew her every move; he'd been sniffing after her like some malevolent bloodhound. God damn him, anyway! 'I know they'd be very interested in learning how you crashed Dale Hessman's plane,' she threatened, 'how you tried to kill me –'

'Please feel free,' Devlin laughed. 'I'm sure they'd be happy to make your acquaintance. Ruth Marx has quite a record – prostitution, drug selling, quite a record.'

So that's what they'd done to her! Not only given her a false identity but also turned her into a criminal. A wave of nausea rolled over Angela, but she fought it back. Her chin came up. 'Yeah, almost as good a record as Bergstrom has, huh? I know all about Bergstrom's suicide, and I know all about the Praetorians, too. I'm sure they'd love to hear all about that.'

Angela's words had a profound effect on Jack Devlin, but he had been well trained in his deadly profession. His face remained impassive, showing nothing but his slight mocking smile. If Angela had learned about the Praetorians, that changed the game plan. She would have to be taken alive, brought in and debriefed, by force if necessary, to find out exactly how much she knew, how she had learned it, and whom she had confided in. That meant that killing her would have to be a pleasure postponed. Temporarily.

'Everybody has a button, Angela. And Bergstrom's just happened to be homophobia. All we did was push that button.' Devlin held Angela captive with one hand, while the other began to search through the pockets of her denim jacket. 'You just need to know people well enough to find which button to push. As well as I know you.'

Angela's gorge rose. He wasn't talking about really knowing another human being through sharing of feelings, thoughts and ideas, a meeting of hearts and minds. He was talking about accessing information illicitly through cyberspace spying, and using that illegally-obtained advantage to gain power, to control human destinies.

'I don't have your disk,' she said flatly. 'If I had it I'd give it to you. I don't have it.' Her eyes desperately scanned the pier for a way to escape. She saw only people having a good time, a turning carousel, whirling thrill rides, a large ferris wheel, a silly clown in a bunny rabbit costume.

'It's okay, it doesn't matter,' Devlin said gently, almost tenderly. 'What we need is what's up here . . .' he touched Angela's forehead with the tip of one finger, '. . . so you come with me.' Delicately he pulled the front of his jacket open a little, just enough for Angela to see the heavy butt of the dark pistol tucked in his waistband.

'I'll take care of you, Angela,' he whispered, like a lover. 'I promise I'll look after you.' With one arm around her, so that they appeared to be just another happy strolling couple, Devlin began to lead Angela off in the direction of the parking lot.

Angela's eyes darted around her. In terror, she looked for help from any direction, finding nothing.

She needed time, more time! 'I don't understand,' she stalled. 'Screwing with airports, stock markets – what is it you people want?'

Suddenly vehement, Devlin swung her around. 'It's not about what *I* want,' he shouted. 'It's about what my employers want. Take a look around you.' He made a contemptuous gesture, a wave at the mobs of happy people. 'Do you think things are working? They believe they can make things better.'

'How, by killing people?' Out of the corner of her eye Angela could see, only a few yards away, the bunny clown dancing a polka with one of the merrymakers.

'I don't ask too many questions. And I suggest that you do the same!' Jack Devlin's cool mask cracked a little, revealing a glimpse of the merciless killer under the smooth façade. Angela wasn't fooled for a minute about what he'd really meant when he'd promised to 'take care of her'.

Suddenly the dancing rabbit, all six feet of him, hopped right into Angela and Devlin, waggling his ears. Angela reacted like a bullet shot from a pistol. She whirled and tore away, pushing the rabbit into Devlin's arms, and ran like hell.

For a moment, Devlin and the bunny circled around each other, Devlin trying to follow Angela and the rabbit clown trying to engage him in a cha-cha-cha. At last, with a savage punch and a furious 'Get the fuck away from me!' Devlin broke free and set off in pursuit.

Angela fled in terror, running as fast as she was

able to, without actually knowing where she was going. Up ahead of her was the carousel, a noisy merry-go-round, every horse taken by a laughing child or adult. Carousel music played, the brightly-painted ponies bobbed up and down, lights flashed; to Angela it looked like a confusion she might use to throw Devlin off her heels. She ran hard, pelting for the carousel, and leaped on it even as it was gaining motion, ducking down behind one of the stationary horses.

Jack Devlin pushed and shoved his way through the crowd, following the direction Angela Bennett had taken. As he ran, he pulled his 9mm pistol from his waistband. He didn't want to kill her now, but given the choice between his shooting her and his letting her get away from him, Angela was a dead woman. He'd blow her away without blinking an eye. He caught only one glimpse of her disappearing into the hordes of people, running in the direction of the carousel.

The carousel? It seemed to Devlin that it was an unlikely thing for Angela to do, to try to blend into crowds and noise. Angela Bennett hated both, was afraid of both. And yet, as he ran he began to think it not so unlikely after all. Angela had changed a lot. Nothing like looking down the barrel of a gun to make a girl re-evaluate her former phobias. He'd go for the carousel. Possibly she thought he wouldn't dare to fire into a crowd. If she believed that, she didn't know Jack Devlin.

Angela raised her head slightly over the back of the colourful carousel horse, and saw Jack Devlin closing in on the merry-go-round. She saw his 9mm pistol in his hand, and she knew he was ready to use it. She looked around desperately for a hiding place, but a moving carousel doesn't offer many decent opportunities for cover.

Devlin eased around the ride, looking for that dark red hair and that denim jacket. There! There she was, reflected in one of the mirrored doors that covered the central machinery, crouching down. He had her now. The ride was now whirling around too quickly for him to jump on, but as soon as it began to slow down, he'd be on it. No matter how agile Angela was, she was no match for his training. He'd be on the damn merry-go-round many seconds before she could get off.

The ride began to slow, just a little. Grabbing a brass pole, Devlin launched himself, his feet hitting the carousel floor. Good. He moved swiftly between the bobbing horses and the waving, laughing riders, his eyes scanning every movement for a glimpse of Angela. But he saw nothing. She had apparently vanished. The ride was now slowing down, and children were already being lifted off the merry-go-round horses. Suddenly, he knew where she must be. Hiding in the core of the carousel, behind the mirrored glass, inside with the mechanisms that turned the ride. One of the mirrored doors was slightly ajar. *Angela, Angela, you can't hide from me.*

With his gun drawn, Jack Devlin pushed the door open the rest of the way. Nobody. The space was empty. She'd been there, and now she was gone. He scanned the departing riders, but could see no trace of her. Angela had gotten clean away. Fuck! *Fuck!!* Devlin kicked savagely at the glass, which shattered. Then he set off to find her. Back to square one. But he'd find her; as smart as she was, as ingenious as she was proving to be, Angela couldn't get away from Jack Devlin and the Praetorians. With their resources there was nowhere she could run, nowhere she could try to hide where they couldn't locate her. But they'd have to find her very soon. Angela already knew too much. Devlin narrowed his eyes in thought. He had some idea of how she was planning her escape. It would be a positive pleasure to catch up with her . . . and shoot her through her pretty little head.

Dirty, exhausted, Angela finally reached the hospital. Escaping from Jack Devlin had taken everything out of her. She had to get away, get up to San Francisco. The answers were there, at Cathedral Software, the answers that might save her life and give her back her identity. Her mind was racing with possibilities, and threats lurked behind every face she saw. If the Praetorians found out about Cyberbob, if Devlin knew exactly where to meet her in Santa Monica, then obviously her hotel room, the telephone there, and her laptop computer were already compromised. She couldn't go back there, and couldn't take her computer with her. She had to get out of town as quickly as possible.

But first she had to see Alan Champion one more time, to say goodbye and, just as important, to ask him to lend her his BMW for the four hundred mile drive up to San Francisco. Ever since she'd driven him to the hospital a couple of hours ago, she'd had the car keys in her pocket, but she didn't want to strand Alan in the hospital without an automobile. He'd be going home tomorrow. Also, she wanted to see his face one more time. Finding Alan again, learning that he still had feelings for her, was the only bright spot in this whole damn horrible business.

Angela was well aware that what she was about to attempt was more dangerous than anything that she'd encountered up to now. She was intending to enter the home territory of the enemy, a well guarded territory; she was about to confront on their own turf a power-hungry group that had already proved they would stop at nothing, that they were ready to kill anyone who opposed them or stood in their way.

What was it Devlin had said about the Praetorians? 'They believe they can make things better.' But they believed it with the arrogance all totalitarian dictators possess, that hubris which makes them believe that they and they alone are capable of making choices for everyone else, even against the people's will. Government with the consent of the governed isn't merely a lesson in civics, it's what democracy is all about. Angela believed that with all her heart and soul.

But now that she was here she realized that walking in through the front door was not the smart thing to do. Angela circled the hospital warily until she saw a lighted exit door around the side. She slipped in, and, avoiding the elevators, climbed up the stairs to Alan's floor. There were some suspicious-looking men hanging around; were they waiting for her or were they merely here to visit friends or loved ones? Angela couldn't take the risk. She flattened herself against the wall, waiting for an opportunity to sneak by them, then she made a dash for Alan's room.

Alan Champion's hospital room was a scene of noisy chaos. Code Blue. A crash cart holding emergency equipment was standing in the middle of the floor, and doctors and nurses were crowded around Alan's bed. One doctor was using defibrillator panels on Alan's bare chest, shouting 'clear' as jolts of electricity made the patient's body buck upward off the bed. A nurse was injecting a strong stimulant directly into Alan's veins. In the centre of all the turmoil lay Alan Champion, his face chalk white but oddly peaceful. He was dead, and all the efforts made to resuscitate him had failed.

'Alan!!' yelled Angela frantically, forcing her way into the room.

'Get her the hell out of here!' shouted the angry chief resident, and two nurses grabbed her by the arms and rushed her out of the room, closing the door behind her.

Stunned, shaking with grief, Angela stumbled over to the nurses' station. 'I don't *understand*, you all told me he was going to be fine. He *was* fine!'

The nurse looked sympathetic. 'We did the best we could, there were complications . . . the insulin . . .'

Insulin? 'No, penicillin!' protested Angela.

The nurse shook her head decisively. 'No, Dr

Champion was being held for treatment of diabetes. He went into insulin shock at – '

'He wasn't diabetic!' yelled Angela furiously and helplessly.

'I'm afraid he was.' The nurse turned to her computer, typing in an access code. 'I could pull up the patient's file, and . . .'

The computer. The goddamned murdering computer. *It had killed Alan!* Acting purely out of the instinct of rage, Angela Bennett lashed out and swept the computer off the desk, sending it crashing to the floor. For a split second she felt a great satisfaction, but then a tsunami wave of grief and fear washed over her again. She was alone now, totally alone. Whoever she'd turned to for help – Alan, Cyberbob – was dead. And she'd probably be next. Jack Devlin seemed to have eyes and ears everywhere; he was linked into his own powerful network whose reach seemed to be infinite.

Even here, at a city hospital, Angela could feel spying eyes on her. Everybody was watching her. It was true; all eyes had turned to the distraught young woman who'd just noisily trashed a hospital computer. But Angela didn't stop to think of that. She ran without thinking as fast as she could out of the exit door and down the stairs, around the side of the parking lot and threw herself behind the wheel of Alan Champion's BMW. Peeling rubber, she tore out of the lot.

For the first five minutes she drove aimlessly, wanting only to get away from the hospital and from the sight of Alan's white face and motionless body. Then she realized that she had to find a place to hide and sleep. It was a good eight-hour drive to San Francisco, up a busy inland highway, and she was in no shape to start tonight. Without sleep she'd never make it.

The first rays of the morning light came in through the window; Angela's lashes fluttered and she half-raised her eyelids. It was very early. She wasn't quite awake yet. Then her eyes opened reluctantly. Where was she? For a moment or two she felt totally disoriented, then slowly the events of the past few days came back to her. Oh, God! It wasn't a nightmare; it was real. She was still living it.

A sudden tapping on the glass made her jump and sit up. Outside the car window a security guard was tapping on the windshield. He was telling her to move it, that she didn't belong here. Angela nodded and turned the key in the ignition switch, and the car roared to life. She drove off the front lot of the BMW dealership where she'd parked all night, blending in as just one more dark BMW in a lot filled with them, hiding in plain sight.

As she headed for the freeway, Angela tried to work some of the kinks out of her neck and shoulders. Sleeping all night in the front seat of an automobile was murder on the muscles; she was as stiff as a steel door and she ached all over.

The roads were slick; it had begun to rain. The BMW, a masterpiece of Teutonic engineering, usually hugged the road with ease, but as the rain began to pelt down heavy as hailstones it wavered a bit in its lane. The freeway was close to empty at this hour of the morning; in less than two hours the heavy rain added to the normal run of Los Angeles traffic would have this road bumper to bumper. She could make real time now; later it would be a lot more difficult.

Suddenly, shrilly, the car phone rang. Angela looked down at it in sudden fright, realizing who must be calling. He knew where she was; he always knew. She didn't want to pick up the phone, but she knew it would go on ringing until it drove her crazy. So she grabbed it. 'Hello?'

'You have no idea what it does to me, just hearing your voice,' purred Jack Devlin.

Angela uttered an oath and moved to hang up the phone.

'No, don't hang up, Angela,' Devlin said hurriedly. 'This is important. If you would just take a step back from all of this, you'd see that you and I are not so very different.'

What is this bullshit? Angela thought angrily. What does he want from me now? Does he know I'm on my way to San Francisco? Yeah, sure, he probably has my position triangulated. I never should have picked up this damn phone. The rain beat furiously against her windshield; even with the wipers going it was becoming difficult to see the road. Traffic was getting a lot heavier now. The closer she came to San Francisco the more cars joined the road north.

'We're both isolated,' Devlin's voice went on relentlessly. 'Both untrusting, both looking for that clarity. You've come to mean a great deal to me –'

'Well, you mean shit to me,' snarled Angela, concerned with keeping the BMW on the right side of the double line.

'I have to admit an arrogance in my perceptions of you.' Devlin's voice dropped to a low insidious murmur. 'You see, I've come to visit an old friend of mine, a *piano teacher* friend of mine –'

Oh, God! Where was that bastard Devlin calling from? The nursing home Oaktree Manor, or the County Sanitarium? Was her Mom still safe? 'You leave my mother alone,' Angela interrupted grimly.

'Ah, well you see, she's been moved by Dr Champion, the *late* Dr Champion.'

He hadn't found Mom yet. Angela felt relief, followed by real anger. The bragging bastard! He murdered innocent people like Alan and Cyberbob and then he boasted about it, like some hunting animal. And all to throw a scare into her! With loathing, Angela punched the 'cancel' button, and the line went dead. But Devlin's latest sadistic phone call totally unnerved her, and she began to speed up. Without her being conscious of it, the BMW's speedometer passed seventy on its way to eighty miles an hour.

On the other side of the road, a state highway patrol car passed the speeding BMW, clocked it at eighty, did a U-turn in the rain and began to tail Angela. She saw them in her rear-view mirror, but what she didn't see was the verification of Alan Champion's car licence plate coming up on their in-car computer. 'Reported Stolen', ran the check from the mainframe database. Now they were chasing a car thief as well as a speeder.

Nervously, Angela checked the rear-view again. The patrol car was definitely coming on fast. Suddenly, an authoritative voice, magnified over a loudspeaker, cut through the sound of the tyres on wet pavement, and the beating of heavy raindrops on the windshield.

'Driver, this is the Highway Patrol. Reduce speed, pull over to the side of the road, and turn off your engine!'

Glancing into her rear-view mirror, Angela gnawed at her upper lip. If they stopped her now, everything she'd achieved so far would come unravelled. She was now only about one hundred and twenty-five miles south of San Francisco. Only a couple more hours would do it. She decided to make a run for it. Instead of reducing speed, she stepped hard on the gas pedal, and the car shot forward.

Ahead of her, Angela could see a large truck hogging the northbound lane. The road was curving at that point; if she pulled out into oncoming traffic, she'd never be able to see what was coming in front of her. But she knew what was coming behind her; the patrol car was definitely in pursuit. She began to drive defensively, weaving in and out of traffic, trying to get ahead of the truck, but falling back again and again as oncoming cars appeared ahead of her. At last she made a definitive move and pulled out from behind the truck into the southbound lane, looking to pass.

Suddenly, a car loomed up in the lane about thirty yards away. Angela swung the wheel hard, but the wet road was as slick as glass, and she lost control. The speeding car fishtailed, hydroplaned across the teeming surface, crashing through a barrier on the shoulder and a road sign, barrelled across a grassy field and came to a wounded stop.

At the same time, the police cruiser pulled off the road, and the two state troopers got out at a run, scudding across the slippery grass and mud to the BMW. The lights were on, the windshield wipers were working away, and the car's front door on the driver's side was open, but the driver wasn't inside. Blood on the seat and on the windscreen told the officers that she couldn't have got far.

Angela ran across the field, blood pouring from her temple, her heart pumping painfully, her legs aching. She almost fell down a rocky embankment, but managed to land on her hands and knees, scrambled, wobbling, to her feet and started to run again. As she ran, she gasped out loud, like a litany, like something precious she had to hold on to very tightly. 'My name is Angela Bennett ... my name is Angela Bennett ... my name is Angela Bennett ... my name is Angela Bennett ... Angela Bennett.' And then the police reached her.

'Freeze!' yelled one of the officers, but Angela kept going. He grabbed her, threw her to the ground with her face in the mud, shouting in her ear. 'Get down! Get down! Put your hands behind your back!' The other officer began Mirandizing her. 'You have the right to remain silent ...'

Angela dimly heard the reading of her legal rights; she could feel the cold steel of the handcuffs pinching her wrists behind her, but everything was moving away from her very quickly, down a long tunnel into blackness. She drifted into unconsciousness.

7

Her head was throbbing so painfully that Angela could barely stumble through her booking, finger-printing and mugshots. While she was being body-searched by a hard-handed policewoman, the arresting officers entered her prints into the California law enforcement database, which soon came up with a match. The alleged auto-theft perpetrator was one Ruth Marx, 39 Admirals Way, Venice, California, with a record of prostitution, treatment for venereal disease, arrests for robbery, larceny, shoplifting, assault, soliciting, drug sales and heroin use. Mother dead of a heroin overdose; no brothers or sisters. The file listed outstanding arrest warrants, including one recent one for parole violation.

The young public defender assigned to her sat across a table from Ruth Marx, shaking her head dubiously. This girl in the orange prison jumpsuit, with her large, wild eyes, the wound on her forehead, her split lip, her mud-streaked hair flopping into her face, looked and acted way out there, zoned in some paranoid Neverland. Or was Ruth Marx, who kept denying that she *was* Ruth Marx, simply lying to get herself psychiatric treatment instead of jail time? With her record it was a definite possibility. *Why do I always get these wacko losers?* she moaned to herself. Yet, on the surface the young attorney's demeanour remained as cool and professional as it ought to be when consulting with a new client.

'Look, I want to help you, I've been *appointed* to help you, but what you're saying is just so far-fetched. 'They' changed your name, your friend's medical records, 'they' crashed planes . . . ?'

'Just think about it,' Angela said wearily. 'Just think about it. Our whole world is just sitting there in the computer. Everything, everything known about us is in the computer. DMV, health records, credit cards, social security – everything is stored in there, a little electronic shadow of each and every one of us, just begging to be screwed with. And you know what? They've done it to me. And you know what? They're gonna do it to you.'

'Look, Miss Marx – "

'I'm not Ruth Marx,' protested Angela again, sighing heavily. 'They invented her and put her on *your* computers with *my* thumbprint.'

The court-appointed public defender sighed in echo; she decided she would take a rational approach although she was pretty sure it wouldn't work with this crazy woman. 'I hate to tell you this, but the California Criminal Justice computers, all of them, have been protected by the Gatekeeper security program for the last six months. Nothing like what you're describing could ever happen.'

Protected by Gatekeeper? Why did that name keep

cropping up again and again? Suddenly, the realization hit Angela. 'Oh, my God! It's the program, then. The Gatekeeper program's got a flaw. If they changed my identity, it's got a flaw, and the Praetorians know this.'

'Well, that solves it,' said the lawyer wryly, 'Now, you want to tell me again how you ended up in a stolen car?'

'Okay, okay, listen to me.' Angela tried to contain her excitement so as not to freak the woman sitting across from her, looking at her with such evident doubt. 'It's like a Trojan Horse, this thing. The Praetorians. They hack into computers and they control things. They cause chaos. LAX, Wall Street – they do this so the people go out and buy this program, Gatekeeper. They buy this program and they get a false sense of security. Only they've let the Praetorians have free and exclusive access into their systems, like a Trojan Horse. Imagine what they could do with this power . . . they could do anything!'

The public defender shut her eyes and drew in a deep breath. No matter what she said to Ruth Marx, this woman would twist it until it fitted in with her paranoid delusions. 'This is all very fascinating, Miss Marx –'

Angela leaned across the table, and the intensity of her gaze burned into the young lawyer. 'Please, my name is Bennett. Write it down. B-E-N-N-E-T-T. Bennett. I have no reason to make up a story like this.'

The PD was coming to the end of her patience. 'As your court-appointed attorney, I'm obligated to carry out whatever you want,' she snapped. 'I'll call you Cleopatra Queen of the Nile if you wish, but take some advice. If you go before the judge with this craziness, I *guarantee* you will be found incompetent to stand trial, and they will hold you . . . indefinitely.'

It was a no-win situation, and Angela Bennett knew it. How could anybody believe her? Why should they? If someone – say, somebody like Cyberbob – had approached her with a cockeyed story like this a month ago, she would have labelled him weirdo and sent him on his way. She knew how she must sound to this young attorney, really off the wall with her conspiracy theories. Just another paranoid nut, but a nut with a long criminal record who'd just been caught in the stolen BMW of a dead man. Nobody here would believe a word she said, nobody. She was effectively up the creek, and the Praetorians had swiped her paddle.

Angela's only chance was to prove that she was not Ruth Marx, that she was really Angela Bennett. But how? There were only two persons in the world who could identify her as Angela Bennett. One was Jack Devlin. The other was her mother, who hadn't recognized her daughter in months. Terrific, an Alzheimer's patient with a fried brain was her one hope. Talk about your irony. Still, she was allowed a phone call. Who else was she supposed to call up, Jack Devlin? *'Hi, Jack, it's Angela. Guess what? I'm in jail. Want to come down here and tell them who I really am? No? Okay, then. You can take another vacation. No reason for you to bother to show up and blow me*

146

away. My life is fucked anyway. They think I stole Alan's car. Nobody believes a word I'm saying, so I'm going to rot in prison until I die. Have a nice life, Jack. B-bye.'

No, call Mom. Besides, she wanted to hear her mother's voice, to know that she was still safe, and to tell her goodbye. God only knew when she'd see her Mom again. Or *if*.

Angela slumped anxiously against the jailhouse wall while she waited for the County Sanitarium to put her through to her mother. Under her breath she breathed a little wordless prayer, *please, please, please.* Maybe Mom was having a good day today! Maybe she'd remember! But Angela wasn't counting on it. 'Hi? Hi, yes, this is her daughter.' She waited some more, nibbling on her lips, until she heard her mother's familiar soft voice, tentative and flat because of the disease that was stealing away her mind.

'Mom, hi, it's me ... it's me, Angela. How're ya doin'? Are you doin' okay? Is that new nurse treating you well? It's *Angela*, Mom! Mom, listen, I need you to do something for me. I have a lady here, you have to tell her I'm me, all right? I'm going to put her on the phone and I need for you to tell her it's me ... No one believes me, so you have to tell them. Can you do that? Mom? Are you there? It's *Angela*!' Tears began to roll down her cheeks, tears of sadness for her mother's condition, of misery for her own terrible predicament. It was all so hopeless. No cure for either one of them.

'I love you, Mom. I just want you to know that I

147

love you,' she whispered, and hung up the phone. For a long moment she stood huddled by the wall, then slowly, she sank down to her knees, her arms wrapped tightly around her body, and wept out loud, wept as though her heart was breaking, which it was. She was so alone. Nobody had ever been so alone. And there was no way out. She had come to the end of the road.

For an hour or so Angela slept dreamlessly, curled like a baby on the thin jail cot mattress, without a blanket or a pillow. Her sleep was created out of the same profound blackness that had inundated her soul; she slept because she was exhausted; she slept because she was heartsick; and she slept because there was nowhere she could escape except to the black country of oblivion.

It was still night when a female officer came into the jail, carrying Angela's clothes, and rapped on the bars of Angela's cell. 'Lady.'

Angela moaned in her sleep and stirred a little. 'Hey, lady, wake up,' the officer said again, tapping more loudly.

'What? What's the matter?' muttered Angela thickly, still half asleep.

'Someone's here to get you. Get dressed.'

Angela sat up, now fully awake, her heart pounding in terror. 'Who? Who's here to get me?' she demanded, but her jailer would say nothing more, just watched her phlegmatically while Angela pulled her clothing on with trembling fingers. As she was led from her cell to the front desk of the police station, Angela was still resisting, trying to dig in her heels, but being dragged along by the jailer's greater size and strength. 'Who the hell are you turning me over to?' she kept yelling.

'Here she is,' the officer said to the desk sergeant, who was busy wrestling with three phones ringing at once. The sergeant didn't answer, but handed over Devlin's wallet and the few possessions from Angela's pockets. 'Sign here.'

Angela looked wildly around her, expecting to see Jack Devlin appearing around any corner. Instead, she saw a tall, goodlooking black man in a raincoat, holding out an identification card for her to check.

'Special agent Ben Phillips, FBI,' he told her. Angela stared back at him, confused. 'Alan's friend,' he added in a low tone. 'It was terrible what happened to him. He was a good friend.'

An enormous feeling of happiness washed over Angela. The cavalry had galloped up with bugles blaring! She was saved! She'd forgotten all about Ben Phillips, but now she saw him as her way out. 'I'm so glad you're here,' she cried, weak with relief.

Phillips threw her a friendly, sympathetic glance. The kid looked as though she'd been through hell and back. 'Two seconds after Alan told me your story,' he said, smiling in reassurance, 'half the Computer Crimes Division hit the bricks chasing this down. Most of them were beating every bush from here to eternity just to find *you*. I'm sorry it ended up in a place like this.'

Angela shook her head at his apology; all that wasn't important now. The important thing was that he believed her, that there were others who believed, who knew her story was true, and that they'd help her to get her life back again. 'So what do we do next?' she asked him.

Ben Phillips smiled at her warmly. 'First, let's get you someplace safe,' he said, signing the desk sergeant's release papers. 'We've got a field office about forty minutes from here.'

'Then what?'

'How about a little fishing trip. Does a shark named Jack Devlin ring any bells?'

Devlin. The FBI knew about Devlin and was going after him. Angela thought she'd never heard more beautiful words. Cheerfully, she followed the agent out to his car.

Ben's car was a standard government issue sedan, inconspicuous, not expensive, but customized with major power under the hood. Gratefully, Angela buckled herself into the passenger seat. As they drove, the FBI man filled her in on Devlin.

'He's their one-man dirty duty squad – smart, efficient, lethal, with the moral conscience of a chainsaw,' he told her. 'But as scary a sonofabitch as he is, the guys behind the keyboards are worse.'

'The Praetorians?'

Ben Phillips nodded. 'We've been chasing them for years. This is our first good lead. But we have to move ASAP here, so start sketching me some quick background. Like how the hell you accessed their system in the first place.'

'I didn't,' Angela explained. 'It was a programmer at Cathedral Software. He just sent me the software disk.'

The agent threw his head back and laughed. 'Oh, man! A goddamned disk, that's what kickstarted all this?' He looked over at her. 'Angie, Angie, tell me, you make any copies? I mean, before it was ruined?'

Instantly, Angela went cold all over, exactly as if she'd been thrown into an icy bath. 'No,' she said quietly, but her blood pounded in her ears, and she looked around the car for some way to get out fast. For the first time, she noticed where they were. The sedan was driving through an area of warehouses and docks, almost deserted and very dark. Surely the Federal Bureau of Investigation field office, no matter how local or understaffed, was housed in some decent federal building in a neighbourhood which at least had coffee shops. Even the most drastic government budget cuts wouldn't set the FBI down in a slum like this one.

So far, the man beside her didn't notice Angela's suspicions; he had no idea that anything was wrong. 'Damn,' said 'Phillips'. 'That disk's the only hope we have of catching these bastards. Did you talk to anybody, give copies of the disk to anyone?' He tried to keep his tone casual.

'God, you amazing sons of bitches,' whispered Angela bitterly. 'Amazing, amazing. *Amazing!* How did you know the disk was ruined? I never said anything about its being ruined. I never said *anything*!'

The man made no reply; he kept his eyes straight

ahead and his hands firmly on the wheel. But his lips were now pressed together tightly and the muscles in his jaw twitched. From his expression, Angela could tell that he knew he'd blown it. She was in terrible danger, but it didn't stop her; it didn't even slow her down. She was too damn mad to slow down.

'What's your name?' Angela demanded. 'You're not with the FBI, you're not even Ben Phillips. Ben Phillips is probably lying dead right now. Who the hell are you?'

There was still no answer, but the driver narrowed his eyes and the car picked up speed. And Angela knew with a sudden cold certainty that he was taking her to Jack Devlin. In fact, as he turned the next corner she could see a lone dark car, which she recognized even at a distance as Devlin's car, waiting for them at the far end of the road at right angles to the curb, blocking the street.

'You bastard. Ever since I first touched that disk I've been running from one damn nightmare to the next. You know, I'm so tired, I'm out of it . . . I'm so out of it . . .' Angela slumped in her seat as though defeated. 'I'm too damn exhausted to be scared anymore. So, you know what? I'm not *going* to be scared! Fuck scared! My participation in all this bullshit is now officially *over*! I'm not gonna play your game anymore. I'm taking my life back! Starting right *now*!'

Suddenly, without warning, Angela made a dive for the steering wheel, at the same time slamming her foot down on the accelerator. The car leaped forward like a jack rabbit as 'Ben Phillips' swore loudly and struggled to regain control of the vehicle.

'Get off it! Get off!' the big man yelled. 'Are you crazy? You'll kill us both!'

'Fuck you!' Angela gasped, breathing hard. She had nothing to lose; any which way she looked at it death was waiting for her at the end of the street. She fought him off with an effort, but she was aided by the swerving of the automobile, which shook the big man from side to side like a rag doll.

The car zigzagged down the dark, slick roadway. It had stopped raining, but the pavements were still slippery and wet. Ahead of her, at right angles to the curb, Jack Devlin's car was waiting for them. Angela aimed the sedan straight at him like a battering ram.

A frantic struggle was going on inside the sedan for possession of the wheel and the gas pedal. As strong as the tall man was, Angela had the advantage of surprise, agility and, even more, of desperation. She was fighting for her life and she fought with animal ferocity. Keeping her foot pressed down on the accelerator, at the last minute she unsnapped 'Ben Phillips's' seat belt.

Devlin gaped in astonishment as the sedan came barrelling down the street straight at him, weaving like a drunkard from side to side. He switched on his ignition key, intending to get out of there fast, but the engine coughed, stalled and refused to turn over.

'Shit!' he yelled, but it was already too late. The sedan was skidding right into him. With a terrible grinding sound of metal twisting, the two cars collided. 'Ben Phillips's' car slammed into the side of

Devlin's, spinning the two vehicles around and smashing them up on the curb. The hood of the sedan crumpled up like paper, blocking the windshield. Devlin's car, being more expensive, was more strongly built and suffered less damage, but Devlin himself was shaken up and bruised. He staggered out of the car, his gun in his hand, looking for Angela.

The hood was so crumpled that it blocked the windshield. Devlin couldn't see through it; he had to go around to the front seat of the sedan. The door on the passenger side was open, and Angela Bennett was nowhere to be seen. The big man who'd called himself Ben Phillips was lying with his head back on the seat, a large gash opened in his forehead and blood oozing from it. He was breathing hard. With a moan, he tried to get out of the car, but he couldn't. He fell back gasping on the seat. Without a moment's compunction, Jack Devlin shot him in the head. The bungling asshole.

Angela ran like a rabbit, down the wet industrial road toward the river. Ahead of her she could see a bridge, the kind of industrial drawbridge that opens in the middle to accommodate the tall smokestacks and radar masts of commercial river traffic. She knew that 'Ben Phillips' wasn't dead, she'd heard him groaning. And she doubted that the crash had done for Jack Devlin; you can't kill the devil. He was a cat with nine lives. Any minute now he'd be coming after her. She increased her pace, even though her side was aching, and the muscles in her thighs and calves protested loudly.

Devlin got back into his car and swung his wheel around hard, smashing into the sedan and forcing it into the wall of the nearby warehouse. He broke free, gunning his motor hard, his tyres screeching as he sped down the street after Angela. His eyes darted this way and that like lasers; if anything moved, he'd see it. His face was grim; this had ceased to be amusing a long time ago, and he was getting tired of Angela Bennett's cleverness.

Angela finally reached the bridge, and scrambled on to the bridge roadway. Lights were flashing, and a steady warning *peep peep peep* noise told her that the drawbridge was preparing to open. In the river below her, Angela could see a trawler about to pass under the bridge; it had a tall radar tower that wouldn't go through unless the bridge opened. Behind her she could hear the roar of a car engine, and she knew that Devlin had spotted her and was coming on fast. She had to get to the other side before the bridge opened all the way. If she was trapped on this side with Devlin, it would be the end of everything. She'd never get away from him.

Now the warning was louder, and the automatic barrier began to come down behind her. Other cars had stopped outside the bridge, respecting the barrier, willing to wait. But not Jack Devlin. Angela turned and took another frightened look over her shoulder. She could see his car barrelling past the stopped cars, breaking through their line. Devlin might have to drive his car straight into the barrier, but Angela didn't doubt for a moment that he would.

The bridge split in the centre; the two halves of the draw began to pull apart, and the bridge itself began to rise upward, making Angela scramble on her hands and knees, as though she were climbing a hill. By now she was close to the centre, but the split was getting larger every minute as the two sides of the drawbridge were pulled further apart. She'd have to jump for it. Behind her Jack Devlin was driving at breakneck speed; below her an icy dark river yawned. Ahead of her was a leap over a widening chasm. Some choice.

Closing her eyes, Angela Bennett braced herself and leaped. She flew through the air and came down with both feet on the far side of the bridge. For a moment her sneakers teetered on the slippery metal, looking for purchase, but she gripped her toes hard and bent her knees, and slid down the slope of the opening drawbridge. She was on the other side.

Standing up, she took a quick look behind her. Devlin's car was still speeding on; it crashed through the wooden barrier, reducing it to matchsticks, and roared on to the bridge. He was going for it; he was really going to try to jump his vehicle, like a stunt man in some chase movie, over the opening in the drawbridge.

Jack Devlin gunned his motor, the car took a leap forward, and Angela, watching it, uttered an unconscious scream. But at the last minute, Devlin slammed on the brakes. The bridge opening was too wide; he'd never make it. His car came down on the wrong side, its front wheels spinning on the other edge of the draw, like a cat hanging from a tree branch with its front paws hooked over.

Angela's legs felt rubbery and she almost sank to her knees in gratitude and weariness. But she pulled herself together and moved on. She couldn't stop now. She had to keep walking, even though all her muscles screamed in protest and her feet were getting numb. It was a lot colder now; she wrapped her damp denim jacket around herself more tightly, but the chill wind off the river cut through the thin fabric and pierced her skin with icy fingers. What she needed most was a hot drink, a hot bath, and somewhere to lay her aching head. As though to underscore her discomfort, it began to rain again now, a hard, frigid downpour.

But Angela kept moving; she didn't dare stop. At last, a couple of dozen blocks from the bridge she saw a small motel with its 'Vacancy' sign lit. Angela fumbled in Devlin's wallet, counting the money. Less than thirty dollars left.

'I'm not driving,' she said to the bored, dumpy woman behind the office desk. 'And I can't pay much. How much for one night?'

'Thirty-five.'

'I can only pay twenty-five. Cash.'

In answer, a key was pushed across the desk, and a rather grimy hand reached out and seized the crumpled bills. Angela let herself into her room and looked around. Not too bad, really; better than she'd expected. It was cheap and it was ugly, but so what? There was a television set, a rather lumpy bed, clean towels in the small bathroom, two tiny cakes of soap, and enough steam heat to make the room stifling.

What more did she need? Angela clicked on the TV, finding a news station, and ran a hot shower, stripping off her wet clothing and draping it over the single chair.

Angela stood under the shower for a long time, letting hot water stream over her tired body and through her hair. One cake of soap she used to wash herself with, the other for shampoo. At last she felt relaxed and clean enough to come out of the shower. Wrapping a towel around her body, she stood in front of the steam-misted mirror, rubbing away the condensation.

For a long long moment she stared at herself in the water-beaded glass. Her reflection shocked her. She looked like a battered woman. Her lower lip was split and there were scratches and bruises on her face, which had grown so thin that her eyes stared back at her, larger than ever. It seemed to Angela that in the last two weeks she had aged five years. Would she ever get her identity back? Would she ever be able to lead a normal life again? Or would Jack Devlin catch up with her finally and put a bullet through her skull?

Here she was, an ordinary person caught up against her will in an extraordinary and deadly situation, in possession of secret information about a worldwide conspiracy. She never asked for this, but she was stuck with it now. So why didn't she just try to disappear? Maybe make a run for Mexico, get a job in a restaurant? What on earth made her think that she alone could take on a group as large and murderous as these Praetorians evidently were? She must really be as crazy as everybody else thought she was.

But she couldn't stop now. She'd come too far. Her life was already at risk; if she didn't continue, her death would be totally without meaning. Mechanically, absorbed in her thoughts, Angela drew her comb through her wet hair. She hadn't been listening to the TV news, but now the anchor uttering a single word . . . 'computer' . . . broke into her absorption and caught her attention. She went into the bedroom and sat down on the foot of the bed, her eyes on the screen.

'On a more serious note,' the anchor was saying, 'after a month of what has appeared to be playful computer tampering, an incident has taken a darker turn. We go to Chicago and Dermot Conley for the report.'

The screen changed from the studio to a remote feed outside the Illinois First State Bank, where reporter Conley stood looking solemn. 'Police report that computer errors turned ugly today when six of Chicago's major banks were forced to shut their doors due to massive computer tampering, bringing the economic life of this city to a halt.'

'Jesus,' breathed Angela, her eyes glued to the screen.

'It is a desperate situation,' the reporter continued. 'essential city services will be conducted through the one local bank unaffected by the glitches. That bank – National Fidelity, sources say – was protected by Gregg Systems' aptly-named Gatekeeper program. Reporting live from Chicago, this is Dermot Conley. Over to you, Ed.'

'Thank you, Dermot,' the studio anchor took over. 'In related news Jeff Gregg, billionaire founder of Gregg Systems, was in Washington for today's announcement by newly-appointed Undersecretary of Defense Calvin Schumaker that the Pentagon will be outfitting the entire federal government with Gregg's touted Gatekeeper program.'

Another puzzle piece fell into place with a click. 'Oh, my God!' she gasped aloud. 'That's what it's about! Total access to the government.'

Angela had been thinking that the Gatekeeper had been somehow faulty, which had allowed the Praetorians to access the program and use it for their own ends. But she'd been wrong, dead wrong. She knew that now. It was far, far more insidious than she'd supposed. No, the Gatekeeper and the Praetorians were in the same plot together, *one* plot, *one* conspiracy, and all the resources of Gregg Systems were used by the Praetorians, who were dedicated to one thing and one thing alone, world domination, beginning with the United States government, to which they had just been handed unlimited free access.

There's an old folk saying, Angela thought: 'Don't send the cat out to buy cream.' Another piece of folk wisdom goes like this: 'Never put the fox in charge of the henhouse.' Here's the analogy: assume you intend to secure your home against burglars, and you hire a security firm, which comes to your house and installs a sophisticated alarm system. Only what you don't know is that your security firm is run and staffed by burglars, who are now totally familiar with the layout of your every room, know where the valuables are kept, and exactly how to bypass the system which protects you, because they installed the system themselves and they have all the security codes. Whenever they choose, they can break in without detection and help themselves to the jewellery and the silver.

That, in essence, was the Gatekeeper, the fox in charge of the henhouse, the cat sent out to shop for cream. A firm of high-tech burglars. But they were not interested in your wife's heirloom brooch or the family silver. What the Praetorians would steal, using Gatekeeper's technological expertise and total access, was your power, your company's control over its own little portion of the universe. They would add your power together with all the other power they had stolen, until they had achieved their primary goal, which was not to lick up your cream or eat your chickens, but to gain complete dominance over the world.

'Ironically, today's announcement came just two weeks to the day after the suicide death of Schumaker's predecessor, Michael Bergstrom, a vocal opponent of the Gatekeeper program.'

'They did kill him,' breathed Angela. And now she knew why. He'd stood up against the Praetorians and Gatekeeper. Now the design of the puzzle was becoming terrifyingly, totally clear. Through a glitch in the Mozart's Ghost disk Dale Hessman had accidentally stumbled into an interface with Gatekeeper. He didn't understand it fully, but he had caught on enough to recognize that here was something potentially lethal to everything and everybody. So he'd died. He'd brought in Angela Bennett. She was supposed to die, too, but Devlin had been careless so she'd got lucky. Cyberbob Fox was on to something, and he, too, was dead. So was Alan Champion, and so was the real Ben Phillips, no doubt. And how many others? How many more in the days to come?

Angela stood up and dropped her towel, reaching for her clothing. She couldn't stop to sleep, she had to get to San Francisco right away.

But, as she was dressing, the news broadcast continued, and Angela turned in surprise to look at the screen. The female anchorperson had taken over.

'Turning to local news, a spectacular car crash leaves one unidentified man dead, with a gangland-style gunshot wound to the head. We go live to the scene of the crash, where Lynn Blake is standing by.'

Angela stared in horror as she recognized the sedan, a crumpled wreck. But 'Ben Phillips' was alive; she had left him alive and moaning. Who had put a bullet in his head? As soon as she asked herself the question, she knew the answer. Jack Devlin. The cat with nine lives.

A handsome young black woman holding a hand mike was talking now. 'Thank you, Elaine. I'm standing just yards away from where the body was found. The police are looking for the passenger of the car, a young woman in her twenties, brunette, and believed to be wanted on federal charges of car theft, who goes under the name of Ruth Marx . . .'

With horror, Angela saw a woman's face filling the screen. Her own face, the police mugshot. Now Homicide would be after her, too. Now she'd soon be wanted for murder. She sank down on the foot of the bed, staring hopelessly into space.

8

It was late in the afternoon but the sky was already dark with overhanging rain clouds when Angela Bennett dropped down from the truck cab onto the street in downtown San Francisco. Painted canvas banners were stretched over the street, announcing an AIDS Awareness walk and candlelight vigil that night. She turned back to thank the driver; after many long, tedious hours of hitch-hiking he was the only one willing to stop and pick her up, and he'd been a surprising gentleman, even though he had filled the truck's cab with choking, nauseating smoke from his hand-rolled Bull Durham cigarettes.

For close to three hours they had been riding together side by side in complete harmony, saying little. Angela relaxed to the country music on the radio and allowed herself to become entranced by the hypnotic white line on the road as it stretched in front of her. Three hours of nothing to do but wait. It might be the last peaceful respite she would ever know in this life. But as the truck rolled over the Golden Gate Bridge, all of Angela's anxieties returned with a vengeance. The task she had set herself loomed ahead of her, to penetrate Cathedral Software's offices and access their systems without being detected. Now it seemed virtually impossible, an amateur climber attempting to scale Mount Everest.

Speaking of Mount Everest, Angela stared up at the glass and steel skyscraper that was the address of Cathedral Software. It was much higher than she'd imagined. And Cathedral itself was huge; it filled the entire fifth floor of the building. Even though she always knew that Cathedral was no Mickey Mouse operation, somehow Angela had always pictured it as homey, downsized and user-friendly, maybe because her dealings with Dale Hessman and Russ Melbourne had always been so pleasant and laid-back. Now she saw, as she looked through the glass doors, a rabbit warren of work station cubicles filled with tekkies, all hard at labour on keyboards, all of them with intent, serious faces. More importantly, Angela saw a security desk just inside the door, and knew that she could never get in there past the receptionist. She'd have to find another way.

Angela retreated to the corridor, to give herself time to think. She was here to penetrate the office and get on one of those computers, but how? She scanned the hallway, noticing an unmarked wooden door about twenty feet along the corridor from the large glass entrance doors, and surmised that this was a kind of employees' entrance. It had one of those simple number locks; press the right four digits in the right order and you were inside. If you didn't know the combination, it might take hours. Angela knew that she couldn't be spotted out here in the hall messing around with different number combinations. Maybe if she waited . . .

Sure enough, within three minutes a man came down the corridor carrying a box of files, stopped outside the door, pressed four digits and pulled the door open. As it swung shut behind him, Angela moved forward swiftly and silently, following him in. She squeezed herself in just before it clicked shut. So far so good.

She attracted no attention. Most of the employees of Cathedral Software were roughly her age, computer nerds in their twenties, dressed as she was in casual jeans and sneakers. The office was a beehive, with worker bees swarming everywhere. There were banks of copiers, printers, fax machines, and much coming and going between work stations. Angela didn't stand out from the rest of them as she roamed around in her search. She found herself in a vast space, broken up by rows and rows of small cubicles, each of them with at least one online computer, monitor glowing. She scanned the ranks of stations, looking for an empty one she could use. But all of them seemed to be filled. When anyone came in her direction, Angela turned aside so that her unfamiliar face would not be noticed, and she would not be spotted obviously looking for something.

A voice came over the public address system. 'Attention, employees. This is a reminder that volunteers are still needed to staff our booth at the Pan-Pacific Computer Conference at the Moscone

Center. All those interested in assisting please call Personnel at extension 5378.'

Over there. That station was empty. Angela prayed that whoever usually worked there was out sick for the day and not just loitering in the bathroom. She slid inside and sat down in front of the computer. Switching it on, she studied the menu on the screen, and when she saw Mozart's Ghost.net, she sighed with relief. 'All right,' she said, calling the file up with a mouse-click. At once, she heard the opening strains of *Eine Kleine Nachtmusik*, and saw again the familiar little guitar-riffing skeleton.

And then, SERVER ACCESS DENIED. RESTRICTED ACCESS. ANGELA BENNETT ONLY, warned the monitor.

'Don't do this to me,' muttered Angela, frustrated. 'I *am* Angela Bennett.' But you can't argue with a computer, so she consulted the menu again, clicking on 'Terminal Echo'. This was the program she'd told Alan Champion about, the one that is able to go back in time and trace old keystrokes. With this program she would be able to call up the files on the disk that had been destroyed in Mexico, the proof she needed to get her life back again.

TERMINAL ECHO SUSPENDED. It was not a welcome message.

Angela nibbled at her lip. All right, she must be sitting at a station with a low security clearance, one that couldn't access the echo program from its own computer. But somewhere on this floor there was at least one fully-authorized computer which could interface with anything its little microchip heart desired, including the echo program. And she'd stake her life that computer belonged to 'Angela Bennett', the woman who had taken over her life and her name. She had to find out which work station was the imposter's, then somehow get her the hell out of it so that she could take over her terminal and access its functions. No easy job. She'd have to take it one step at a time.

To access the echo itself, the user had to possess an authorized terminal identification number. Angela called up a map in the echo program, which displayed the location of all work stations by number only. From the map there was no telling who worked where.

First, she had to pinpoint 'Angela Bennett'.

She picked up the phone and dialled Cathedral Software's number. When the receptionist answered, Angela asked for Angela Bennett. Somewhere in the vast workspace she could hear a phone begin to ring, and then it was picked up.

'Programming. Angela Bennett,' responded a woman's voice. Angela said nothing but, pressing the phone tightly to her ear, she stood up in a crouch, just high enough to see over the top of the partition. Her eyes scanned everywhere, looking for a woman on the telephone.

'This is Angela Bennett,' the woman's voice came through again, sounding irritated. 'Who the hell is this? Look, if you've got something to say, say it, otherwise . . .'

'Don't hang up,' Angela said quietly. She knew she was taking a big risk, the risk of being discovered herself, but she mustn't lose this call, not until it gave her a fix on the terminal she needed.

'Angela?'

There was a pause, and then the imposter did a very foolish thing. She stood up and peered over the top of her work station, searching for the real Angela. 'Angela Bennett' was young, dark-haired, and looked quite a bit like the genuine Angela, resembling her in height, weight, the way she wore her hair. She was even wearing jeans, like Angela. And she was quite nearby, only a couple of work stations away.

Gotcha.

Angela sat down at the computer again and clicked twice on 'Angela Bennett's' terminal number, 5E12. Her monitor showed 'Terminal Suspended' changing to 'Terminal Active'.

But the imposter knew in the same instant that she'd been identified. And she also knew that the real Angela Bennett must be inside somewhere, not very far away. How the hell had she penetrated the security of Cathedral Software? Her face creased with worry and doubt. She placed her fingers on her keyboard, typed in a hidden password, called up the Mozart's Ghost.net program, and accessed 'Praetorians'.

'SUSPECT ANGEL IS NEAR. ADVISE IMMEDIATELY!' she typed.

A small smile tugged at the corners of the real Angela's lips. 'All right, Ms "Bennett",' she muttered, 'now that I know where you are, let's see if we can get you away from your machine.'

Back to the keyboard. This was her element, this was where Angela Bennett was a star. She selected a program from her menu that provided her with a schematic of the building in which Cathedral Software's offices were located. She mouse-clicked in on the fifth floor, the Cathedral floor, then on the fire detection system, finding herself a conveniently nearby alarm station. 'How about if I started a little fire ... right here?' she mused aloud, pointed and clicked, triggering the computerized fire alarm.

At once, the overhead lights all over the floor went out, and every monitor in the company began to issue fire alarm warnings. There was an immediate hubbub as the computer analysts popped out of their cubicles in the dark, and milled around buzzing, exactly as bees do when the hive is disturbed. Was it a real fire? Was it only a drill?

All except 'Angela Bennett', who sat at her terminal, still waiting for instructions from the Praetorians.

'Hey, Angela, who are you, Our Lady of Asbestos? We have a fire here.' The floor supervisor, who was also the company's fire warden, looked in on her, sounding annoyed.

'Yeah, yeah, yeah, just give me a sec.'

'No "give me a sec". *Now!*'

Reluctantly, the imposter closed down the program, left her terminal and followed the supervisor to the fire exit. Under cover of darkness, the real Angela Bennett slipped inside the work station and sat down at the computer. She quickly called up Mozart's Ghost again, and was rewarded with a screen that declared, 'Welcome, Angela Bennett.' *Well, it's about time somebody acknowledged me.*

Immediately, Angela clicked on the little *pi* icon, and her screen told her that this program was protected by Gatekeeper Security. Then, as though to belie that protection, it rapidly scrolled through columns of figures and diagrams and brought Angela right into the program of the Atomic Energy Commission. But it demanded an authorized password, and Angela didn't have one.

All right. Let's not sweat it. It's got to be in here somewhere. She recalled the menu, and clicked on the terminal echo program. There, as though reading a carbon copy, Angela found the password she was looking for, 'nairo.23ae'. She typed it in, and was again rewarded. The imposter 'Angela Bennett' evidently had Level D Guest Access Remote Security, and her terminal was at once provided with a brand-new menu Angela had not seen before.

She studied the choices it presented. On it, among such listings as Bethesda Naval Hospital, Internet Airline, US Passport Office, Cathedral Software, even the pharmacy which had filled Alan Champion's fatal prescription, she read the names of Ben Phillips and Angela Bennett. Angela felt a swell of satisfaction. She had found what she'd been looking for. Angela mouse-clicked on her own name, and immediately her face and her identity as Ruth Marx filled the screen.

For the first time, Angela came face to face with the

police record that the Praetorians had dreamed up for her. The arresting officers had not made her privy to it; why should they? They presumed that Ruth Marx must be well acquainted with her own past history. With horror, Angela read that she had dropped out of high school at fourteen, that she had a long series of arrests for misdemeanours that had escalated into felonies – heroin use, prostitution, shoplifting, burglary, assault. She read that she had been treated for venereal disease and heroin addiction, that she was a parole violater and worse. She scanned her mother's drug rehab history, her mother's death from an overdose – it was too much. Sickened and furious, she clicked on 'Delete', intending to wipe this shameful record away forever and regain her life.

Instead, she read the message on her monitor: YOU MUST HAVE MAINFRAME ACCESS TO DELETE FILE.

Damn! The loud wailing of fire engine sirens caught her attention. Angela stood up and went to the window, pushing the blinds aside, looking down at the sidewalk. Fire engines were coming down the street. At the far corner she could see the AIDS parade already in progress, as with candles burning the demonstrators made their slow death-march down the broad avenue. In front of the building, the workers from Cathedral were standing puzzled, looking up to see if they could spot flames coming out of the fifth floor.

Angela knew that 'Angela Bennett' was among them, and she knew, too, that as soon as the fire fighters reached this floor she'd be out of time. They would identify the whole thing as a false alarm, and it would be business as usual. The Cathedral programmers and analysts would soon be returning to work. She'd have to get out fast, without what she'd come for, and it was unlikely that she could make a successful second attempt. And now that she had actually been face to face with Ruth Marx's criminal record, Angela Bennett was determined not to leave here until she had deleted that file.

Suddenly, Angela heard the buzz that signalled an incoming message on her computer. She ran back to the work station.

TERMINATE ALL MOZART'S GHOST FILES NOW, she read. TERMINATE ANGEL NOW. And it was signed, PRAETORIAN.

Down in the street, fire fighters were beginning to roll out their long hoses and carry them into the skyscraper. 'Angela Bennett' demanded of a fire official, 'If there's a fire, where's the smoke? There's no smoke!' The imposter knew that something smelled fishy here; the worst case scenario was that the real Angela Bennett, code name Angel, had penetrated the building's computerized systems and 'started' the fire, and was even now up there gaining access to computer files that were none of her business.

The message from Praetorian sent Angela off on a new inquiry. WHOIS PRAETORIAN? she typed.

At the 'whois', the program entered its search mode. The screen provided Angela with no name or address, but there was an IP number: 23.75.345.200.

'Search IP23.75.345.200,' she typed. Immediately, a long set of strings appeared, a complicated series of sets and subnets. Whoever Praetorian was, he was hiding his identity under pathways and packets that often came up with empty screens. Nevertheless, Angela's computer went on tracking, matching digit after digit one at a time. It was a slow and laborious process.

Without warning, the overhead lights came back on, and Angela realized that her little sham fire drill was over.

'Attention,' announced the public address system. 'The fire department has determined that there is no fire. This is a false alarm. You may return to your offices.'

She was running out of time fast. The Cathedral Software employees would be on their way back any second, and she was sitting here at 'Angela Bennett's' computer, where she had no right to be. If they caught her, they'd turn her over to Security, and Security would turn her over to the San Francisco police. Once the police had her, their computers would tell them that Ruth Marx was wanted for questioning in the murder of an unidentified man, and it would all be over.

But she was so close, too close to give up now. Only a few more digits; the computer had already matched 23.75.345, and was still working on the final 200.

The Cathedral workers began to file back into the building. 'Angela Bennett' tried to get into the first

174

elevator going up to the fifth floor, but it was full, and the doors closed before she could push her way inside. While she was wasting time doing that, a second elevator left without her. But she was on the third.

The last three digits were matched. MATCH DETERMINED. LOOKUP COMPLETE. An Internet e.mail address and photograph scrolled down, and Angela found herself looking into the face of Praetorian himself. He was Jeff Gregg. 'So you *did* do this,' she murmured aloud.

All at once, the last puzzle clicked neatly into place, and she saw the entire monstrous design clearly and in its entirety. It was obvious. Why hadn't she seen it before? This was not a conspiracy by the Gatekeeper and the Praetorians; they weren't in on it together. They didn't have to be. Gregg Systems and the Praetorians were one and the same. It was Gregg Systems behind *all* of it, and the Praetorian himself was Gatekeeper's creator. God, it was so simple, and so terrifying. Now she had the proof.

No, scratch that. She'd *seen* the proof, but she didn't actually *have* it, not where it would do her any good. Angela needed to get it on disk – all of it, the files that proved they'd been behind the LAX and Wall Street and Chicago bank debacles, behind the suicide of the Undersecretary of Defense, the files that proved how they'd killed Dale, and Alan and poor Cyberbob, the files that proved how they'd changed Angela into Ruth Marx. It had to be in her hand, on a disk, not just up there on the screen. Downloading a full and complicated set of files like this into a copy program would take time, even with the fastest hardware. And time was the one thing Angela didn't have. Any minute now all of Cathedral Software would be walking in through those glass doors, and 'Angela Bennett' would be with them.

Time was on 'Angela Bennett's' mind, too. The elevator seemed to her to be crawling up to the fifth floor. At this rate, Angela would own the company. 'Come *on*!' she muttered, showing her impatience visibly. A co-worker smiled at her with empathy. 'You have to go to the john, too, huh?'

Where the hell were the blank diskettes? Angela rummaged through the stuff on the imposter's desktop, finding nothing. The imposter had to have backup disks somewhere; you can't run a computer without them. She pulled the top drawer open. And there she found two things. On top was a photograph of Dale Hessman and his family, which she pushed aside without curiosity, because she had never met Dale and didn't recognize any of the people in the picture. But under the photo was a FedEx envelope with her own handwriting on it. It was addressed to Dale.

She looked inside. She found Mr Depina's red virus disk, the one Angela had sent Dale for his collection of the world's worst computer viruses. For the first time, she realized that 'Angela Bennett's' work station had been Dale Hessman's. The ironic revelation made her shiver. But she couldn't stop to think about that now. She shoved the virus disk into her pocket and rummaged further in the drawer. Thank God! A blank formatted disk. She slammed the blue diskette into the A drive and hit 'Save'.

SAVING FILES, read the monitor.

The elevator doors opened and the Cathedral people began filing back into their offices. Angela looked around desperately. She could see men and women swarming down the corridors in her direction. Any second now she'd have to get out of here, but she couldn't, *wouldn't* leave without the precious backup disk. The disk was the only proof she needed; it was the reason why she was risking everything to be here.

'Angela Bennett' marched swiftly toward her office. She was tempted to break into a run, but she didn't dare call so much attention to herself. Her face was grim. She expected to be confronting Angel at any moment.

There was a peep from the computer. The files were now safely stored on the blue backup disk. Angela snatched it out of the computer and hurried out of the work station, moving in the same direction as the other workers, blending into the crowd. She slipped out of the side door and into the corridor. Security guards were posted by the doors, so Angela ducked down a side corridor, looking for an inconspicuous way to get out.

She noticed a fire fighter up on a ladder, his head disappearing into the ceiling panels as he checked for a possible short in the alarm system which might have triggered the false alarm. At the foot of the ladder were his helmet and his rubberized jacket.

But in her rush to get away from Cathedral, Angela had made one mistake. She should have turned off the imposter's computer. Then nobody would have been able to assess the actual depth of her penetration of Gatekeeper. They wouldn't know for sure that she had unmasked Jeff Gregg himself.

The minute 'Angela Bennett' saw Jeff Gregg's face and Internet address on her monitor she knew exactly how far Angela had gone. All the way. She read the words, 'Copying Completed' and knew that Angel had even made a copy. The imposter's face darkened, as she grabbed up the telephone and dialled the extension of the building security police.

'Security. We've had a break-in on the fifth floor. We're looking for a woman, about five feet seven, dark hair . . .'

That was probably a waste of time. By the time the guards started looking for her, Angel could be out of the building and on her way to the FBI. She had to be stopped another way. 'Angela Bennett' slammed the phone down and ran out into the corridor looking for Angel. She noticed a loitering pair of security guards, one a woman.

'Did you see a brunette?' 'Angela Bennett' demanded breathlessly. 'Did she come by here?'

'Nobody came by here.' The female guard shook her head.

'Sorry ma'am,' added the man. 'The only people coming and going by here are the firemen.'

Of course, the clever little bitch. She was disguised as a fire fighter, like a book hiding on a bookshelf. The imposter pulled her cellphone out of her purse and punched in the number of Jack Devlin's car phone.

'Devlin? Get here *now*! Angel's been here. You've got to take her out.'

Devlin uttered a profanity and slammed his car into gear. This time he would get her. This time Angela Bennett would not get away. With murder in his eye, he approached the Cathedral building, but was forced to stop and park his car a block away, thanks to all the fucking confusion kicked up by the AIDS parade and Angela's false alarm. He finished his journey on foot.

As he ran up the steps, Devlin's eyes raked the crowd from side to side, looking for the slight figure of Angela Bennett. He bumped into a smallish fire fighter in helmet and fireproof jacket, who was emerging from the building with a length of hose over his shoulder, but he paid him no attention.

If he had, he would have seen that the fire fighter was the very person he was hunting, Angela Bennett, wearing borrowed garments. With her heart in her mouth, she walked right by Jack Devlin and into the street, mingling with the other fire fighters, who were pulling up their hoses and stowing their gear in their trucks, getting ready to leave.

A moment later, 'Angela Bennett' came running out of the building and up to Devlin.

'Where is she?' he demanded.

'The firemen, she's got to be with the firemen. We've got to find her *now*. She's copied the disk.'

Devlin whirled on her with savagery. 'Well, how the hell did *that* happen? You were supposed to get rid of it.'

179

'And *you* were supposed to put a bullet in her head a week ago,' countered the imposter defensively. 'She should never have been alive to make that copy!'

They both stopped short, falling silent. At the base of the steps were a fireman's jacket, neatly folded, with a helmet placed on top.

Devlin grabbed the cellphone from the imposter's hand. 'You better call Gregg. Follow me in the car,' he told 'Angela Bennett' grimly. He strode to the corner, looking in every direction for his quarry. The AIDS parade stretched on for blocks; it was the perfect place for Angela to hide herself, within the protection of a line of marchers. Devlin hopped on a fire truck at the curb so he could see into the crowd. Yes, there she was, he could see her plainly, running against the flow of traffic, pushing her way through the demonstrators.

This was a mistake, no two ways about it. What Angela should have done was join in the line of march, with her head down, maintaining the same slow pace as the others. Instead, she stood out like a sore thumb; Devlin could trace her progress like wind through a wheat field, as the marchers yielded and fell back from her running desperation.

But Angela wasn't thinking clearly, because she had only one thing on her mind. She had to get her proof to the proper authorities; she had to find a safe computer with a modem so that she could transmit the files on the disk. And that meant only one destination. The Pan-Pacific Computer Convention at the Moscone Center, five long blocks away.

180

Devlin raced through the line of AIDS demonstrators, keeping his eye on Angela, who kept bobbing up ahead of him, now disappearing into the crowd, now showing herself plainly. Then she veered off and ran down a side street. Jack Devlin followed her; a suspicion had begun to form in his mind. If he knew Angela – and by now he was certain that he knew her well – then he knew where she would be headed. To the nearest computer with a modem. Over the last weeks Devlin had watched Angela change from a timorous, easily manipulated and life-avoiding girl into a sharp, ingenious and courageous young woman. Until now, with that disk in her possession, Angela Bennett was a human time bomb. He had to stop her. Devlin increased his pace, breaking into a flat-out run.

Out of breath, Angela reached the front steps of the large convention hall and looked up at the building sign: the Moscone Center. Above it, a banner was hanging, 'The Pan-Pacific Computer Convention, Welcome to the Future Today'. She dashed inside, not seeing Jack Devlin running hard about a block behind her.

Devlin pulled out 'Angela Bennett's' cellphone, and dialled his car phone. 'She's going into the Moscone Center,' he reported to the imposter. 'Meet me there.'

The computer conference was packed with a record turnout of visitors, business people, computer professionals and amateur hackers wandering from booth to booth, watching the exhibitors' demonstrations and picking up freebies – computer books, cloth shopping bags with company logos, free software. The aisles were jammed with people. Angela pushed into the crowds without even being aware that they *were* crowds. She saw salesmen and saleswomen demonstrating computers everywhere she looked, but there was no way that she could simply step into an exhibitor's booth and sit down at the keyboard. No, she needed a full bank of computers, with at least one of them free and online, and hooked up to a modem. She needed to come off like the average convention visitor, playing hands-on with a company's hardware. Most of all, she needed to be left alone to do what she had to do.

Devlin met up with 'Angela Bennett' on the mezzanine level overlooking the convention floor. They stared down at the throng. It was a mob scene. There were hundreds of exhibitors, thousands of visitors. 'Jesus, she could be anywhere,' said the imposter. 'Are you sure she's out there?'

'She's out there, all right,' Devlin answered with a bitter smile. 'She won't be hiding in some corner. She's here to use a computer.'

At the far end of the convention hall, Angela spotted the Cathedral Software exhibit, one of the largest at the Moscone. Up on a platform at the far end of the hall there was a bank of Cathedral computers, most of them empty. The salesperson manning the booth was out of the way, busy talking with a potential customer. Angela hurried to the platform, and sat down at one of the computers. She didn't notice Jack Devlin and the woman who had stolen her identity scouting the perimeters of the hall, searching for her.

Angela leaned closer to the screen, lost in her work, accessing Cathedral's applications menu. She mouse-clicked on 'Electronic Mail' and 'Change Server'. Now she was in. On the next menu she scanned down to 'FBI Department of Justice' and 'Bennett, Angela'. The computer was hooked up to a modem, and accepted the electronic mail command. The screen scrolled. Yes, now she was accessing the Department of Justice mailbox, FBI division. Quickly, Angela typed in her message.

'I have been witness to serious crimes committed by, and on behalf of, Jeff Gregg, the founder and president of Gregg Systems,' she keyboarded. 'Attached to this message is evidence of these facts.'

On the convention floor, Jack Devlin was grimly closing in, getting closer and closer to the Cathedral Software exhibit. He was as angry as he'd ever been in his life. Angel should never have been allowed to penetrate this far, never! Again and again, she'd gotten away from him, hitting him where he lived, in his pride. Her survival to this moment reflected badly on Devlin and his methods, which up to now had always been murderously efficient. She had ruined his perfect record. Oh, he would enjoy watching her die, he really would! Angela Bennett's death had become a matter of restoring Jack Devlin's wounded ego. He checked every booth on the way, seeing no sign of Angela. On the other side of the computer conference hall, the imposter 'Angela Bennett' was closing in from the other direction.

The only sound that Angela heard was the muted clicking of the keys. The only thing she was aware of was the unfurling of the words on the monitor in front of her. They told her to 'Insert Diskette'. Angela mouse-clicked on 'Send mail'. She pulled the blue disk from her pocket and shoved it into the model drive, backwards. Damn it! She pulled it out again and stuck it in the right way, hitting the keys that would upload its files into the telephone hookup with the Justice Department. 'Your mail has been sent,' read the screen.

It was done. The FBI now had it all, tangible proof that the Gatekeeper system was set up only to obtain power over all government institutions, proof that the suicide of the Undersecretary of Defense was actually set up by Jeff Gregg in order to install a security program in the federal government, one that only he could access. The FBI now had proof that other murders had followed in order to cover up, that Angela Bennett's identity had been taken away and she had been falsified into Ruth Marx. Now there was only one thing left to do.

Angela pulled out the backup disk, and thrust Dale's red virus disk, the one containing Mr Depina's Wolfenstein XII virus, into the A drive. She reached for the keyboard to hit Escape, the one keystroke that would wipe out the entire Gatekeeper system. But before she could do it, Angela was dragged roughly away from the computer and hurled savagely into the next chair.

'What do you think you're trying to do,' snarled

184

Jack Devlin, sitting down next to her. 'Save the world?'

Angela's chin came up and she looked him straight in the eye without flinching, although she knew that she wasn't likely to live much longer. 'No, not the world, just myself.'

'Too late for that,' Devlin told her coldly. 'The offer's been withdrawn.'

'You might want to look at that screen,' replied Angela. 'Because everything on that disk has just been sent to the FBI. Everything.'

'So?'

'So,' Angela retorted defiantly. 'Now they have proof that the Gatekeeper program has a back door, proof that Bergstrom's and Dale's murders were orchestrated by Gregg.'

'My, my.' Devlin gave her an evil smile that acknowledged her abilities. 'Watch her!' he ordered the imposter, who appeared suddenly on the platform from the other side. Jack Devlin and 'Angela Bennett' circled Angela like a pair of predatory animals.

'The beauty of the Gatekeeper system is that we can get in and out of the FBI as if it were a public library,' grinned Devlin. He tapped on a few keys, gaining mainframe access, bringing up the FBI on the menu, and typing in his own hidden password. 'Beautiful system.'

'Let's finish the work and get the hell out of here,' 'Angela Bennett' said. 'All these people make me nervous.'

Devlin stood up and leaned over Angela, grabbing

her roughly by the hair so he could speak directly into her ear. 'No harm done. Everything you've done will be entirely wiped out just by escaping the system.' He let go of her hair, slapping her hard on her head with a sideswipe blow.

'Really?' Angela couldn't help a covert glance at the virus disk in the disk drive. If only Jack Devlin didn't notice that it was a red one, not the blue backup. If only he would hit the Escape key! *Hit Escape*, Angela prayed silently. *Hit Escape.*

Devlin shot Angela a look of scorn, which said plainly, 'How the hell can you possibly believe you're going to get away with this, you fool? Then he deliberately touched the Escape. Immediately, the screen began to dissolve, the graphics and the lettering disappearing into pixels, like a sprinkling of coloured confetti.

'It's a virus eating through the mainframe!' yelled the imposter in panic. 'Devlin, do something! It's eating through the entire system!'

'Shit!' gritted Devlin. He leaned closer to the monitor, typing rapidly, his jaw working. But nothing helped; even as he frantically attempted to stem the destructive tide, right before his eyes the program continued to disintegrate layer by layer, as though an onion were being peeled and chopped up. What the devil had she done? He looked around angrily for Angela, but she was gone. She'd taken the opportunity to slip away unnoticed while the other two were busy at the computer.

'Take the far side!' he shouted at the imposter, and they both dashed off to find her.

Angela ran through a service door and down the stairs into the mechanical bowels of the Moscone Center, a basement boiler room where the heating system and the central air conditioning units were located. It was dark; only a few low-wattage service lights were on overhead, and they were scattered here and there. Angela flattened herself against a wall and waited, holding her breath, straining her ears. She heard a door open and shut, and she knew it was Jack Devlin coming after her.

Angela could barely make out Devlin moving only a few yards away and she knew that if he detected even the slightest sound or movement it would all be over for her. She heard him coming closer, his light footsteps echoing in her brain as loud as cannons.

Holding his pistol in both hands, Jack Devlin advanced very slowly, one near-silent step at a time, waiting between steps to listen and look. His cat's ears and eyes penetrated the gloom of the boiler room, checking for the smallest rustle of sound. She was in here somewhere; he could sense her fear. This time she wouldn't get away. He owed her, owed her big, and now he intended to pay Angela Bennett off. In full, for everything she'd done to him.

Yes, there she was! Devlin saw a slight movement ahead of him. 'Angela, stop!' he cried out. 'Angela!' He aimed in the direction of the movement and pulled the trigger. The silenced shot thudded into flesh.

The slight figure of a young woman moaned once and collapsed to the floor, lying motionless. Devlin ran forward and turned the body over. It was 'Angela

Bennett', and she was dead. The real Angela was still alive, still in here somewhere. 'Shit!' muttered Devlin.

A sudden movement caught his eye. He whirled around in time to see Angela racing up the stairs to an exit door. 'Angela!' he shouted again, to stop her. But Angela didn't stop, and Devlin fired again. The bullet ricocheted off the stair railing, striking sparks, and Angela disappeared through the exit, running for her life.

She was backstage of the Moscone Center, running through corridors that led she didn't know where. There were exit doors everywhere, but Angela had no idea what they might open into. Any one of them could bring her into a trap, cornering her in some one-way cul de sac with no way out. Something grabbed at her suddenly, pulling her around and making her cry out. Her denim jacket, which Angela had been wearing tied around her waist, had been hooked on an extruding pipe. Angela pulled away, leaving the jacket hanging on the pipe, and dashed on to the next exit.

It had to lead somewhere, because there was a green electric sign over it, 'Exit', and a fire extinguisher hanging beside it.

Her heart thudding with fear, Angela pushed the door open and raced through it. She found herself out on a catwalk, fifty feet above the ground, overlooking a large storeroom far below. At the other end of the catwalk she saw a door, and she ran to it. A sign told her that it led to the electrical room, to mechanical equipment, and to the stairs. The stairs. The way out. She had to get in there.

Angela tugged at the handle with all her strength, but the door wouldn't budge. It was locked from the other side. The only way she could go was back across the catwalk, back toward Jack Devlin.

Devlin prowled through the corridor, searching for some trace of Angela, and he found it. Her denim jacket, hanging from a pipe, told him that she had just passed this way.

Yes, a few feet further along an exit door was standing open, and a long L-shaped catwalk could be seen beyond it. Devlin walked out on it, shoving his gun into the waistband of his jeans.

'Angela,' he called, 'it's just you and me now. Do you realize that you've changed everything? Oh, yes. One little stroke of the key and you've wiped out my employer. Cancelled my contract. You've destroyed everything they've done to you, you've returned your life back. It's what you wanted, wasn't it? Angela, come out. You have nothing to fear from me anymore.'

Angela watched him from the shadows. Jack Devlin stood between her and escape. If she made the slightest move he would see it and shoot her. She was convinced of that, no matter how soft and blandishing his words, he was lying through his teeth. He wouldn't rest until he'd put a bullet in her brain. Hadn't he just killed his own confederate because he'd mistaken her for the real Angela Bennett?

Devlin paced to the L of the catwalk and looked out over the storeroom below, scanning for Angela among the boxes and the electrical and mechanical equipment kept there. Every muscle in his body throbbed with only one desire, to see Angela Bennett lying dead at his feet.

This was Angela's only chance. She was on the long leg of the catwalk; Devlin was standing on the short end. Without looking back she dashed across her leg of the walk through the open door. She heard Devlin cry out her name behind her. 'Angela, come back, I won't hurt you.' The lying bastard.

Devlin sped down the catwalk, heading for the door. Suddenly Angela Bennett appeared in the doorway, silently waiting. Devlin grinned.

'I knew you'd do the right thing,' he said, as he pulled his pistol from his waistband.

In that same instant, Angela's arm swung around, and the heavy fire extinguisher she'd taken from the wall smashed against Jack Devlin's head. His head snapped back, and his eyes rolled up in their sockets and he took one staggering step towards her. Crack! Angela swung the fire extinguisher again, catching Devlin on the other side of the head, the savage blow driving him backwards against the railing of the catwalk.

For one long horrible instant Jack Devlin hung there, the blood pouring from his head, close to unconsciousness. His dazed eyes stared into Angela's and in them she saw a question. The universal question, 'Why?' Then, without a word, he toppled backwards, over the railing, and fell screaming, his arms flailing wildly as his body twisted in the air, to the floor fifty feet below.

Numbly, Angela went to the railing and looked over. Devlin wasn't moving; he would never move again. The cat with nine lives had no lives left. She shivered, feeling suddenly cold all over, and set the fire extinguisher down. Then, slowly, she returned to the convention floor. All she could think of was that the nightmare was over; it was finally over. The odds against her had been enormous; she could have died anywhere along the way. But she hadn't died, she'd survived and she'd won. And only through her own efforts. Nobody had believed her; nobody had helped her. She'd had to do it alone.

Soon they would find 'Angela Bennett's' body, and match the bullet in it to the gun with Devlin's finger-prints. They would know that he was a killer, and the FBI would have the proof of who he was and what he'd done. She'd be in the clear. Now she could leave, maybe get some rest.

Slowly, Angela walked to the Cathedral Software exhibit, and climbed up on the platform. The blue Gatekeeper disk was still sitting near the computer she'd used, and she pocketed it, just in case. For a moment she stood looking silently at the monitor, watching her own face turning into indecipherable pieces of light.

In its final ravages of the Gatekeeper system, the face and record of Ruth Marx dissolved into nothing-ness. Only Angela Bennett was left. And she was going home.

Home to her little house and her garden, and home to the person she loved most. She'd get her mother out of County and bring her to Venice and they'd play Chopin duets again, even if her mother didn't know the notes anymore. What did that matter? All that mattered was the love her daughter had for her. Angela Bennett would be Angela Bennett again, but with a big difference. She had left behind her old fearful, reclusive life, as a chrysalis discards its outgrown covering when it emerges as a butterfly. The new Angela Bennett would fly.